THE SUMMER OF HEROES

by Michael E. Owens

Trinity Press
Atlanta
Published by Scribblers Press
9741 SE 174th Place Road
Summerfield, Florida 34471

Library of Congress
US Programs, Law, and Literature Division
Cataloging in Publication Program
101 Independence Avenue, S.E.
Washington, DC 20540-4283
Library of Congress Control Number: 2020906254

Owens, Michael E. 07/04/2020

The summer of heroes / Michael E. Owens

Summary: In West Texas in the 1870's, 13-year-old Billy's dream of a lazy summer is interrupted when he is forced to take his family's cattle to market when his father does not come home and where he meets many real-life characters on his journey who all become heroes in one sense or another.

ISBN: 978-1-950308-12-5

Acknowledgements

I must thank my parents, Mary and Joe, first of all, for allowing me to spent time in my room writing as a pre-teen when most kids (at that time in history!) were outside, building forts and treehouses, riding bikes and constructing racers, playing with friends and staying out until the streetlights came on. Those many stories I wrote then are now long gone and lost forever in the rubble of my room. (My mother was a clean freak and nothing passed her eyes that didn't need to be tossed – and it was!)

It wasn't until high school did my writing get recognized. Competing against the best brains in my school of 1800 boys at East Jefferson High School in Metairie, Louisiana, I won the Gold Medal Award for Journalism in my senior year. Why I didn't pursue a career in writing as I enter college, I will never know.

In college, at Louisiana College, in Pineville, Louisiana, I was encouraged to continue writing by my history professor, Dr. Thomas Howell. He noted my writings for projects in his class and it gave me the feeling of pride and accomplishment and the germ to build on my writing skills.

As I began my career in the education field, I was responsible for writing many training manuals, instructional books, program plyers and other literature related to special education. Still I did not see me publishing any of the other personal writings with which I was involved.

It was not until my late wife Bonnie encouraged me to think about publishing my work did I begin to buckle down and get serious about it.

Not until my move from Louisiana to Georgia in 2015, and my subsequent retirement, did I find more time to write.

Then, my marriage to Leda the following year was the catalyst that prodded me to make my first novel a reality. With her great support, strong encouragement and sincere inspiration to believe in myself and follow my dream, I am publishing my first novel. She has been with me throughout the process of writing editing, reediting, meeting with publisher and artist, and attending my writer's group meetings every month. Her patience and understanding as I spent hours at the computer writing made my work much easier. I thank her for that. She was definitely my rock.

I also want to thank those closest to me who keep the faith going and were encouragers to me as well. First, my oldest granddaughter, Grace Crouch, read my book and offered her suggestions and corrections. I appreciate her interest in my work. And I give thanks to my children, Kristen Crouch, Kyle Owens and Kelly Owens, who allowed me to move from Baton Rouge and find a new life, find a new dream and to find a new wife. This freedom I found after my move to Georgia and the support of my kids and my grandkids gave me the hope and the future I felt God had allowed me to have.

I want to thank Woody Driskill, a fellow actor with the Phoenix Players, who also is a well-respected retired media specialist (a librarian as we knew them in the old days!) in several counties as well as the Georgia Department of Education. His encouragement was much relished.

Many thanks also to Charles de Andrade, the untiring leader and faithful organizer of the Scribblers'- a Christian writers' group. Our monthly meetings at the Crossing Restaurant in Norcross. Georgia were a not-to-be-missed event for anyone who is a serious published or a would-be published writer. His insightfulness and deep knowledge of the ins and outs of being published helped all of us. I was especially blessed to sit at the table with him and soak in his wisdom not only of the printing business but his understanding of Scripture and Biblical truths.

Of course, I would be remiss if I did not thank my editor, Casey Cox Daniels. I was amazed how much she truly delved into my book and asked the right questions that ultimately made my book a better read and a much-improved story. Her attention to detail surpassed my own knowledge of the words I put on paper. I became a better writer because of her.

And then I must thank my publisher, Trinity Press of Norcross, Georgia, who work feverishly to complete my book for the annual Decatur Book Festival, the largest book festival in the world. Joe Dye and his staff made the process seem so effortless. I want to especially thank Bridgett Joyce for her cover design, and the entire pre-press and press people who made this book possible.

Then there were the countless others whose prayers, encouragement, and inspiration was so vital to my desire to continue my writing journey.

Thanks to you all, and God bless you everyone!

FOWARD

Mike Owens is a true artisan. Not only does he write, but he also creates musicals, and acts in both his own and other works. As a Christian writer, one is often left thinking that writing needs to be spiritual in some way, but Mike finds wonder in the simple things in life, and demonstrates why everyday life should be wonderful to consider. Whether it is a series of poems about the reasons children might give for not liking vegetables, or the stories about cattle drives, and life in the west, or the life of a river boat man, and the trials of the son of the man known as Mike Fink, Mike Owens tells stories that you can visualize and relate to. For Mike, writing is about telling stories, and he does an exceptional job developing the characters and then connecting their lives with his readers. Enjoy his foray into published storytelling, it will be time well spent.

Charles de Andrade
Author
Steward Series
www.stewardseries.com

TABLE OF CONTENTS

CHAPTER 1

A WEST TEXAS SUMMER

"You still talkin' 'bout that horse? You're crazy, Billy! That horse don't even exist!" Thomas laughed loudly. He was just a year or two older than me, and he thought he knew everything.

Thomas and his slimy cohort, Silas, had passed by while I was telling some of the boys about the horse.

"That ain't no horse you see! It's only shadows! Maybe you're seein' ghosts!" Thomas looked around to make sure everyone could hear him. "O-o-o-o! Billy is seein' gho-o-o-o-sts!"

He laughed out loud and all those who had now gathered around us laughed right along with him. No one wanted to cross him so everyone laughed along to humor him, whether you agreed with him or not.

He was a bully and he had always looked for a way to fight with me. My mom said it was because he was jealous of me; jealous that I had a dad who cared for me. Thomas never had a dad that I could remember. It seemed every time I talked about my dad, it would rile up Thomas and he had to butt in my conversation and try to fight me. But jealous? I never could figure out why he would feel that way. But then again, maybe Thomas and I had more in common than I realized. Both of us struggled without our dads around. At that moment, the only thing we had in common was a dislike for each other.

His freckled face twisted as he bared his crooked teeth. I could hardly see his eyes, which were just tiny slits behind the long red hair that covered most of his face.

"Maybe it was a streak of lightnin' you saw flashin' in the desert!" said Silas, Thomas' puny little sidekick who laughed real loud at his own remark. He was not the threat that Thomas was, so no one laughed with him.

By now, Thomas had moved to press his nose up to mine, and again his face became contorted. As we stood face-to-face, I could feel the gathering crowd growing with anticipation. They began to whisper at first, but then grew louder and louder as they chorused together, "Fight! Fight! Fight!" I could feel the eyes of everyone as they darted from me to Thomas, then back to me, and back to Thomas. They were egging us to fight. I wanted to respond, to answer his lies, but at that moment words failed me.

I was never sure how the fight started or who made the first move. The next thing I remembered we were rolling on the dusty ground with our arms wrapped around each other. Thomas' cheek was pressed against mine and I could feel his hot breath on my neck. Our legs were flailing against each other's legs, and it seemed to be our only means of gaining an edge in the fight.

My eyes were full of dust so I could not see who finally grabbed the collar of my shirt. Whoever it was had dragged me away from Thomas. I jumped to my feet and blinked the dust away just enough to see that Thomas was now in the grip of Miss Loganton.

"What's wrong with you two?" Miss Loganton scolded. Her eyes were as big as saucers and as stern as I had ever seen them. "Fighting is not permitted at this school! Not as long as I'm the teacher!" She glared back and forth between both of us. "And don't let me hear that you continued this fight later, or I will keep you after school every day until the end of the year. Do you both hear me?"

By now we had calmed down and were trying to catch our breath.

"I asked both of you a question!" Miss Loganton was serious.

"Yes, Miss Loganton," I answered.

"I heard you," sneered Thomas.

"Thomas! That is not quite the attitude I was hoping from you!" Miss Loganton was still gripping Thomas tightly. She began to twist his collar and he started to choke.

"Yes, Miss Loganton, I heard you."

With Thomas' more remorseful tone, Miss Loganton loosened her grip. "Now, everyone - back to class." There was barely a movement from anyone in the crowd until Miss Loganton shouted loudly, "NOW!"

As the crowd finally started to break up, I looked around to see who had pulled me off Thomas. It was Silas. I was not sure if I should be mad or glad. *Was he trying to save Thomas from me or me from Thomas?*

I tried to shake off the dirt that covered me. Sweat and dust was caked on my arms and face. While I continued to clean myself as best I could, I heard a voice behind me.

"He is real, you know. My daddy told me."

It was Elizabeth Todd, another classmate, still spotlessly clean in the mist of the dust bowl Thomas and I had kicked up. I must have had a puzzled look on my face because she continued:

"The horse, silly. My daddy told me that he is much too wild to be tamed; especially by a person like you." With that remark, she turned up her nose and flung her head around. I watched her long blond curls and her prissy dress flap in the wind as she marched back into the schoolhouse. I dusted myself off some more and followed her in.

I knew there were some who said they had seen him. They also said he was too wild to be tamed. They said horses like him would never be ridden. But I believed I could catch him and tame him and ride him. I would have a name for him too, one day - the day he became mine.

Obviously I had not shaken off all the dust after the fight at school because I heard my mom yell out to me when I approached our back porch:

"You are not coming into this house with all that dust on you!"

I knew from the tone of Mom's voice that she was not playing. She was serious. I was sure she had been cleaning all day and yet the apron around her dress was as neat and clean as the moment she put it on that morning.

"How is it you can go to school as clean as can be, and in just a few hours, come home covered from head to toe in dust?" she asked. "How do you do it?" she added, not seeming to expect an answer.

I answered anyway. "Well, Mom, I guess it is just these hot, West Texas summers and the wind that kicks up so much dust around our ranch. No matter how hard I try, the dust seems to find me." I dared not tell her about the fight.

It sounded like a good excuse to me. As I watched my mom, she glanced at me with a doubtful eye. My mom looked bigger than she really was as she stood there on our back porch. I could see small beads of sweat on her broad forehead, glistening in the evening sunlight. She stood there with a heavy broom in her hand, and I knew if I were to get close enough to her, she would swat me for trying to come in the house so dirty. Her dark brown eyes were set deep in her round, full face. Her complexion always appeared ruddy, like she had been in the sun too long without her bonnet.

Without another word from me, I quickly turned and headed for the barn. I decided that before I washed up, I would take care of my horses.

After checking their feed and water, I headed for the wash shed. It was nothing fancy - just a big barrel filled with rainwater that had drained off the roof of the barn. With such little rain in the last few weeks, it was less than half full. I leaned over and with both hands, cupped the water and splashed it on my face. I dipped my arms in as far as I could go to wash the dust off them. My eyes were closed as I looked around for a towel. Suddenly, I felt one being pushed into my hands. I grabbed it and quickly dried my eyes to see where it came from. I looked down and there stood my little sister, Carrie.

"What are you doing here?" I asked, knowing full well she was sent to make sure I cleaned up well enough to go inside.

"Mom told me to bring you this towel and to make sure you really washed yourself good," she said with a little bossiness in her voice. I was right.

My little sister had always been bossy - with me and her other brother, Daniel. He was two years older than she was, and she would boss him around even more than she would me. Of course, it never bothered neither Daniel nor me.

As I continued to clean myself, I watched my sister. She reminded me of those pictures I would see in some books of those little angels called cherubs, with their little round faces and chubby little bodies; and on her head, she had locks and locks of short, curly blond hair.

My dad had put a small mirror above the wash barrel, and when I stopped to look into it, I heard her declare, "You look a lot like Daddy."

I continued to look in the mirror and I was surprised to see how much I really did favor him. Mom had told me often that we looked alike, but I just figured moms always said that about their sons.

Both of us had thick, unruly tufts of black hair and our faces were long and thin. My skin was not as dark and wrinkled at his. Mine was much smoother. He often had a beard or moustache. However, the closer I studied the face in the mirror, I could see small, dark hairs growing out of my face. It scared me – the thought that I was becoming a man suddenly struck me hard. I realized that I did not need to stand on my toes anymore to see my whole face in the mirror. I was growing taller, too. It gave me a funny feeling to know my body was changing.

My self-evaluation was soon interrupted.

"Billy! Carrie! Supper's ready!" my mom called to us.

Supper? Was it time for supper already? Carrie skipped on ahead of me. I realized that I must have lost track of time. Why was it that at school, the hours went by so slowly and when I got home, the hours were so short? It wasn't fair.

My dad did not go to school like we did, and he did fine and we were not that poor. Many people thought my dad was famous – he had done so many good things for so many people everywhere. Everybody knew him. *So, why did I need to go to school so much?* I was already thirteen years old. The only reason I could figure was that my dad said I had to go and my mom backed him up. Or was my dad telling me because that's what my mom wanted to hear? Of course, I believed my mom was just as strong in mind and body and will as my dad, if not more so. Sometimes I could talk my dad into changing his mind, but Mom - not a chance! Once she decided something had to be a certain way, a body better do it, or she'd get that broom after you. I remembered her telling me,

"Billy, this is 1875. A young man has got to have his schooling in this day and age."

School was not that bad, I guess. I did have a few friends and I really liked learning sums. I was the best in my class. I could cipher numbers in my head faster than my teacher could do them. She reminded me often that I had to let some of the other students answer arithmetic problems a time or two.

Sometimes I liked it when I didn't have to answer. It gave me time to think about my horses. Darlin' was probably my favorite. She was a golden brown with these really long lashes over her eyes. Princess was a good horse, too, but she was much smaller than Darlin'. She was a dark chestnut brown with a very long mane than would sometimes cover her eyes. She was fast, but not as fast as Darlin'. When my dad was here, he always rode Darlin' and I would ride Princess. But when he wasn't here, Darlin' was my horse.

Then there was Whiskers. He was the slowest horse ever! Not only was he slow, but he looked and acted like he was the oldest horse too. He had these long gray hairs sticking out all over his muzzle. That was why we called him Whiskers. These were not the only horses I would think about. Most of the time I was thinking about *him*, the one I had just fought over at school. I did not have a name for him yet, but I would one day. He was the wild one, the great white stallion that roamed the hills in the panhandle of Texas, and especially deep in the mountains outside our town of Ringgold.

Most everyone I knew laughed at me when I told them my dream to make that horse my own. Everyone except Thomas, that is. He wanted to fight about it.

"Billy, this is the last time I'm going to call you!" My mom's voice snapped me back to reality.

I was still standing at the wash barrel. "Coming, Mom," I yelled back, "I was really dirty!"

I grabbed the towel Carrie had given me and I headed back to the house. I thought to myself, *Tomorrow is Saturday. School is almost over. A lazy, easy summer is just ahead.*

CHAPTER 2

SUNDAY DINNER AT THE TURNIPSEED HOUSE

Every Sunday, we always went to church. We got to church so early each week, we were often the first to arrive. It wasn't so bad. I had lots of time to play and I loved the big trees in the church yard. They had lots of low-hanging branches that made them easy to climb. My mom never liked for me to get dirty but she was so busy visiting with her friends, she never noticed I was always playing in the trees. Or did she notice? Maybe this was a time she just ignored it and let me do what I enjoyed.

Another reason I liked church was that sometimes we got invited over for dinner. I guess folks knew my dad was away a lot, and felt sorry for my family. Anyway, different families in the church would invite us to eat with them on Sunday and my mom really enjoyed visiting with them. It was a lazy time for me and the food was always good.

This Sunday, the Turnipseeds invited us to dinner after church. Normally, I looked forward to visiting, but this was going to be different. For one thing, I didn't like the Turnipseeds. They were snooty. They had the biggest house of anyone around Ringgold. I passed by it a few times, but never cared to look at it. They always had fancy clothes - much fancier than most folks do around these parts. They had too much money and they'd let everyone know it, too. I could not believe my mom when she said we were going. I felt like they only wanted to hear gossip about my dad. I knew *that* was the real reason they invited us over. I figured that just like everybody else, they were going to ask too many questions about all the adventures of my dad, whether they were true or totally outlandish, and it would make me uncomfortable. I would think my mom would not want to hear all the wild tales people would rumor about him. But she would always answer everyone with a smile and a laugh. Me? I thought people who asked so many questions were just being nosey. I reckoned the Turnipseeds were like that.

I didn't say too much as I drove the wagon to their house after church. I just listened to Mom talk to my brother and sister.

"Stop fidgeting, Daniel! I want to make sure your face is clean!" She took out a handkerchief and wrapped a corner of it around her finger. As she held Daniel's chin, she licked the end and tried to rub the dirt off his face. When I was younger, I always hated it when she would do that to me.

Daniel looked a little like me, except he was real small for his age. He wasn't much bigger than his younger sister, if that, although he was two years older than her. Most people thought they were twins. He was very quiet and when he and Carrie were together, she did most of the talking for him.

Then my mom turned to Carrie. "Hold still!" she said, and did the same thing to her; wiping Carrie's face with the end of her handkerchief she licked for Daniel. Neither one of them seemed to put up the fuss I did when I was their ages.

"Daniel, tuck in your shirt, and pull up those suspenders!" she said as she tried to smooth out his clothes.

"Carrie, pull up your stockings, and pull your dress down. Please try to sit up like a little lady. And remember, you will not be playing in the barn today," she continued as she straightened out my sister's bonnet.

"Oh, Daniel, look at your shoes! How do you get them so dirty? Use this to wipe off all that dust!" she seemed exasperated as she handed her hanky to Daniel.

She now turned back around in the wagon, but she continued to talk to them. "We will be eating with some very fine people in a very fine house. I want you two to look your best and show your best manners, too."

Just as I was beginning to wonder if she cared how I looked, she added without even looking at me: "Dust off your pants and shirt as soon as you step out of this wagon, young man."

OK, I said to myself, *she noticed me after all.*

We were soon at the gate of the Turnipseed's home. Their house was big. It was too big for just one family, and it seemed to have more rooms than people. It had a second floor. We had two floors in our house, too; we just didn't have any windows on our second floor. We had a porch, too, but not that big, and not with that many chairs and tables and swings and plants hanging and growing along the railing.

As I guided the wagon through the gate, I got a strange feeling. The closer I got to the house, the more uncomfortable I began to feel. The house was set far from the main gate. Many trees were sprawled across the front of the house, and it wasn't easy to see from the main road. I didn't want to stop Whiskers too close to the house. The whole place looked as if it could swallow us up.

Carrie and Daniel immediately jumped out of the wagon and began to play chase around some of those larger trees. They even seemed bigger than the ones in the churchyard. Mom started to yell at them, but just as quickly as she leaned forward to call out to them, she settled back with a sigh.

"Those two will be the death of me yet," she said. Then she glanced at me and said, "And you be on your best behavior, young man. You have made it very clear you do not want to be here, but I like these people and you will not ruin this afternoon for me. Do you understand?"

She sat and waited for a reply. I wanted to argue, but the stern look on her face told me I better just listen.

Sheepishly and reluctantly, I replied, "Yes, ma'am, I understand. I will be on my best behavior, I promise."

With that assurance from me, she turned and waited for me to take her hand and help her down from the wagon. Normally she would have just jumped, but on this occasion she expected me to be the gentleman. I reached out my hand and she took it softly and stepped to the ground. She straightened her apron and bonnet, and with her chin held high, headed toward the front porch.

I didn't plan on misbehaving, but I was not planning on letting the Turnipseeds think I was having a good time either. *Oh, well, I thought to myself, I will try to enjoy this although I know I won't.*

"My, my, my Mrs. Pecos, I wanted to tell you how divine you looked today in church. We are so charmed to have you dine with us this evening," said Mrs. Turnipseed as she walked down the steps of this huge house to meet us.

"Divine?" "Charmed?" "Dine?" Where do you get talk like that? I thought. I guessed that was how they talked in the East. It sounded so funny, I almost laughed out loud, but I had promised Mom I would behave. I guessed that

included not making fun of how anyone talks. I had heard talk like that from a few travelers when stagecoaches would sometimes stop in town. They were people who were headed west to California, I guessed, to make their fortune finding gold. The stagecoach would stop in front of the General Store and the folks would rest a moment. Since we didn't have a hotel, the people never stayed very long. They would buy a few things to eat on the ride while they continued on. The only family who stayed was the Turnipseeds. They didn't need to go to California to find their riches. Mr. Turnipseed stayed and opened our bank. I heard a lot of those people who went to find their fortune in California, never found it and never got rich. The Turnipseeds were already rich before they even got here.

I guessed, when Mrs. Turnipseed said my mom looked "divine", she meant she looked nice. Well, my mom looked as nice as she could for a frontier lady. Mrs. Turnipseed was not a frontier lady. She wore store-bought dresses that were covered in lacy designs and frilly patterns. I didn't know much dress talk, but I could tell they were fancy with matching bonnets and all. Mom's dress was plain and simple, just like all the other ladies in church this morning, except for Mrs. Turnipseed.

I watched the two women as they talked. My mom was big and tall and red of face. The other looked thin, almost frail and her face was the color of fresh milk. My mom's bonnet was plain and just large enough to cover her face from the sun. The other had a bonnet that was much too large for her head. It had little holes all over it, and when she was in the bright sun, the light showed through it and onto her face. It made Mrs. Turnipseed look like she had the spotted fever. I almost laughed out loud again when I thought about it.

"And you are Master William, I presume," Mrs. Turnipseed said as she looked at me down her bespectacled nose. *Master William?* I hated that. "I would shake your hand, but I am sure you have been with those horses of yours this morning already." She continued to speak to me as she turned away and led mom into the house. "The well is in the back. You may use the rear entrance."

I stood there for a moment in disbelief as I watched them enter the house and the door closed behind them. *Didn't my mom hear that? Was I like a slave?* I was mad for an instant until I realized she was right. I was with my horses this morning, but how did she know that? I was supposed to wash my hands when I finished, as my mom always told me, but I remembered I did not. Alright, I decided to wash them at the "well" and I would use the "rear" entrance. I thought to myself, *I tell you now, I will remember this, and I will not like these people - ever! I hope my mom will never come back here again. I knew I never would. And what did "presume" mean anyway?*

Before I got to the well, I began to smell the food. Suddenly, I became very hungry. It was the smell of chicken. When we cooked chicken at home, we would turn it over a fire on a long spit until it was dark brown and dripping. It was ready when the tips of the wings and legs turned black and the skin began to split. It was my favorite. We did not eat chicken often, but when we did, it was a real treat.

There were more smells. I could smell fresh bread, then the smell of baked apples and cinnamon. As I sniffed the dry air, I would think I could smell one thing, but as I drew in more air, it became mixed with other smells coming from the kitchen. The more I tried to breathe in all those wonderful odors, the more they became blended and less distinct. Now more than ever, I was becoming real hungry. Maybe it would be worth the washing and worth using the rear entrance to eat at the Turnipseeds today.

I must have taken longer than I thought. As I entered the back door from the porch, everyone was seated at the table, waiting for me. I saw Mr. Turnipseed standing at the far end of the longest dinner table I had ever seen. Mom was seated at this end and motioned for me to sit on the side next to her. As I slipped into my place with head bowed, Mr. Turnipseed began to pray.

"Heavenly Father, for this bounty, we are truly blessed, oh, God. Allow us to enjoy Your kindness at this table together. Bless these our friends with whom we share our meal today. Amen."

Before I could even lift my head, I heard the clanging of knives and forks and spoons and glasses. I opened my eyes and I saw such a spread of food like I had never seen before. I glanced down the length of the table to the right at all the bowls of food and the large platter of chicken placed in front of Mr. Turnipseed. As my eyes came back the other way, I glanced across the trays of vegetables and hot bread. Then I stopped.

I looked up directly across from me only to see a girl with golden hair and a beautiful face. I had never seen her before, and she was staring straight at me! I had to blink my eyes to make sure I was seeing clearly. Then she smiled and looked away. I didn't move a muscle until I heard Mrs. Turnipseed say,

"Master William, I don't believe you were in the house when I introduced your mother to my daughter. Master William, this is Samantha. Samantha, this is Master William."

There, she said it again! For some reason, I felt embarrassed, yet I couldn't take my eyes off their daughter. Mrs. Turnipseed continued to introduce the rest of the family to me, but I was not listening to her. I was staring at the girl across the table from me. *Where had she been?* I thought I knew everyone in and around this town for many miles. *Why didn't she go to school?* She looked my age. No, she looked younger. No, older. Wait. I was not sure how old she looked. I couldn't tell. Her skin was even whiter than her mother's skin. She looked even frailer than Mrs. Turnipseed, too. As she peered back at me, I swallowed hard and glanced down at my hands in my lap. For some strange reason, I checked to make sure my hands were clean. In spite of being so hungry just moments before, I now felt a lump in my stomach that made me feel very full. I never thought I would ever be short of words, but now, nothing would come out. I felt a nudge on my shoulder, and I faintly could hear my mother say,

"Billy, be cordial. Say 'How do you do?'"

I again looked up at Samantha and I nodded, but I could not take my eyes off her. "How d-do y-you do?" I could barely choke the words out.

"I am fine, thank you," she replied as a broad smile covered her face and, all at once, she seemed happier, and her eyes began to twinkle. I smiled back.

Our trance was soon broken as the plates of food started around the table. In the next instance, the table was full of clatter and chatter and the sounds of laughter and pleasant conversation. Even in the midst of all the noise, my mind was on the new girl about whom I knew nothing, and about whom I wanted to know everything.

I was offered the chicken that the Turnipseed's maid had been cooking all morning. For something that smelled so good just moments earlier, I now had no taste in my mouth for anything. I was very careful as I moved knife and fork and glass for fear of embarrassing myself even more. *Why did I feel this way? Why was it so hard to swallow? Why did every bite I take seem to grow in my mouth? Were my hands shaking?* It wasn't cold. It was summer. I sat in silence as a festive meal played out around me. I remembered nibbling at the chicken and the baked apples as I listened to voices around me talk about my dad. Usually I was very interested when anyone brought up my father's name. There were so many stories about him. Many true and many not true, and many wonderful stories that no one believed could be true.

One by one each of the children were excused from the table - first, the Turnipseed twins, Robert and Rachel; then my brother, Daniel followed by my sister Carrie, who was now best friends with the Turnipseed's youngest daughter, Maggie, who now left to join the other children outside. Next to leave the table was the Turnipseed's two older sons - Clark and Charles. I did not know them at all. They came to town after the Turnipseeds had arrived in town less than a year ago. Their sons just got here last month. Everyone was saying they had to finish school back East. They looked awful old to just now be finishing school. I was already thirteen and I would be finished in just a couple of years. They now worked in the bank with their father. I didn't get to the bank, ever – I had no reason.

Samantha did not excuse herself. I was waiting for her to go and then I would follow. She was listening to the adult conversation, when Mr. Turnipseed called to me.

"You, too, can be excused, William, if you would like to go out with the others."

"No, thank you, sir," I replied as I cleared my throat, "I'd like to stay right here." *For one thing,* I thought to myself, *I was too old for my brother and sister and their friends, and I was much too young for Clark and Charles.*

"Very well, suit yourself," he said. "We are taking Samantha to the front porch."

Everyone rose to their feet – that is, except Samantha.

"Taking" Samantha? I asked myself. Why couldn't she go herself? Did she always have to stay with her parents? Couldn't she decide when and where she wanted to go? Every moment, I was beginning to like the Turnipseeds less and less. The only good thing was that Mr. Turnipseed did not call me "Master" William.

Samantha did not move. She did not get up from the table to go with her parents. In a moment, the cook walked in. I had heard her name being called several times during the meal. They called her Britt and I vaguely remembered someone at the table telling my mom that she was from Sweden. She was a large woman and looked a little like my mom, except her hair was yellow and she wore it long, tied behind her head. She walked up to Samantha and leaned over her and asked,

"Are you ready my dear?"

"Yes," she replied, "I've already unlocked the wheels."

Wheels? What wheels? What did she mean, "wheels"? As I watched the scene unfold, I saw Britt pull Samantha away from the table, turn her chair, and push her to the front of the house. *A chair with wheels? But why?* As they passed out the front door, I felt very alone. The table just sat in silence, and I could only hear the faint distant sounds of children playing and the creaking of rocking chairs and porch swings. I also could hear the sounds of muffled chatter, mixed with laughter coming from the front porch. I could hear someone coming. Maybe it was Britt, returning to clean off the table. I did not want to be seen sitting by myself at the table. I got up quickly from my chair and tried to be as quiet as my surroundings. I had soon eased out the back door.

I saw my brother and I grabbed him as he was racing around the house.

"Daniel," I called out to him in a loud whisper. "Tell Mom I had to go and take care of the horses. Tell everyone goodbye for me."

He nodded and was gone in a flash.

I took off through the fields behind the Turnipseed's home. It was the long way, but I just wanted to get away. As I darted home, I said to myself,

Goodbye, Samantha.

I was sitting at the table eating an apple when my mother and brother and sister walked into our house. My mom's first glance was stern, but quickly turned to a grin.

"Ah! What a divine meal! Aren't you glad we could all dine with the Turnipseeds? And why did you leave for home so quickly, *Master* William?" she said, as she mimicked Mrs. Turnipseed. "You did not tell anyone goodbye and you did not thank the family for a wonderful dinner."

"I told Daniel!" I said, defending myself.

Now her voice had changed, and she was a little more serious. "Was that proper?" She waited for me to answer. I was hoping she would not expect me to say anything. But she stood motionless, and glared at me. I knew I had to say something to her.

"I had to get home to Princess and Darlin'," I said as convincingly as possible.

Without moving her eyes off me, she cocked her head to one side. I knew what *that* meant. It meant she did not believe me and she wanted the truth. Again, she waited.

"It's the Turnipseeds. I just don't like them!" I blurted.

"That's it? That's it?" She paused. "And all this time I thought you were afraid of that pretty little golden-haired girl. What was her name again?"

I looked up to tell her, and I saw her face. She was smiling. I knew she remembered her name. She was trying to fool me.

"Oh, yes! I remember! Samantha." She continued to talk to me as she turned around and began to piddle in the kitchen. "What a bright child! So smart! She read to us, Billy. You missed it. She played the piano, too! You would have liked her, Billy, if you had only stayed."

She continued to talk about the dinner, but I was no longer listening. *Why did I leave? Why didn't I stay?* I wanted my mom to tell me why she was pushed around in a chair with wheels. It was something I did not understand. I wanted her to tell me I was smart, too.

I got up from the table and slowly walked out to the back porch. I didn't even know why I was there. As I walked aimlessly out to the barn, my mind continued to drift back to that "pretty little golden-haired girl", whose name was Samantha. *Would I ever see her again?*

CHAPTER 3

TALKING ABOUT MY DAD

It wasn't until later that evening when I remembered that at the Turnipseed's dinner table I had heard a lot of talk about my dad. I didn't remember much of what was said, and I was now very curious. People were always talking about my dad. Sometimes it made me proud when people would tell me wonderful stories about his different adventures. But then at times, they would tell such awful stories in such ways that it would make me either very angry or very embarrassed. I learned very quickly to tell the difference between those who were our friends and those who were not. I could hear it in their voices, and I could see it on their faces. I could tell when someone truly believed in my dad and when they didn't. Sometimes they told bald face lies just to get my reaction. They would stretch the truth so far I couldn't believe anyone would tell such a tale.

"Mom," I questioned, "what did you talk about at the Turnipseed's?"

My mom was sweeping the floor and humming to herself. She was deep in thought as I watched her. I loved my mom. She never made me feel bad about doing the things I liked to do. She knew what those horses meant to me, and she let me spend as much time as I could with them. She often talked about my dad, but not the way everybody else did. She didn't brag or make up wild stories. She talked about how he loved us and took care of us and how important it was for him to be gone so often and for so long. I knew some of the stories she heard must have broken her heart.

I often heard her say, "Now why would anyone be spreadin' such stories as that? Where could you have heard such a tale?"

She never called anyone a liar. She would say they were telling "stories" or "tall tales", but I knew what she meant. She would quickly jump in and begin to talk about his hard work and being a family man. She never believed the bad things and didn't mind people believing all the wild and crazy things she would hear.

My dad taught us never to brag or boast, unless we could prove our mantle, and then he would say, "If you can do it, you don't need to brag. Others will do the braggin' for you."

I didn't talk about my dad as much as most folks thought I should. When I did talk about him to others, half would think I was bragging and the other half thought I was lying. So, I just let them tell the stories they heard and I tried not to react. Sometimes though, with two scoundrels like Thomas and Silas, I had gotten so mad I had to defend my family and we ended up ready to fight several times. Mom said I shouldn't let others get to me, and that everyone has their own opinion, but it was hard not to take up for my dad. It was funny when I thought about it. The time I finally did have my fight with Thomas, it was over a horse and not my dad.

She was still sweeping the floor when she called out to Daniel and Carrie to get ready for bed. As they scampered back into the house, she leaned her broom against the wall and turned toward me. I was staring at her and she noticed. I must have had that puzzling look on my face as I waited for an answer. It seemed like she always knew when things were bothering me. She cocked her head and leaned toward me, and in almost a whisper, said,

"Were you talking to me?"

"Yes, ma'am," I answered as I shifted around in the chair. With my chin rested in my hands and elbows on the table, I asked a different question than the first. "Why did the Turnipseeds ask us to dinner?"

"Well," she sighed as she sat in the chair across from me, "They are new in town and they are mighty friendly folk. . ." She paused. She knew I wanted the real answer. She tilted her large frame towards me.

"Billy," she began, "you know folks are very interested in your dad. There are few people who don't know who Bill Pecos is. People hear a lot of wild tales about him. Sometimes they want to know if they're true and sometimes they want to hear more. Many people think your father is almost bigger than life. All I know is that he loves you and he loves me. I know you miss him, as do Daniel and Carrie," she paused, "I think you and he have something very special between you. I have seen you with your horses. You have a way with them, Billy. Horses understand you and you, them. I have never seen anything like that before except in one man - your father."

She smiled at me and brushed my forehead with her hand. I watched her as she looked at my face. She ran her fingers through my hair as if to straighten it, and she continued:

"There is many a cowboy who owes his life and livelihood to your father. Many a cattle drive would have failed, and many a settler would not have survived the winters and summers here and all over if your dad had not been there to help. When there is someone like that, someone like your dad, who has done so much and who is known so far and wide, everyone wants to tell a tale of how he helped them. Even folks who don't know him or never met him jump on the bandwagon and retell stories and retell stories again and again, and swear they saw it all! Those folks'll add more and more to the stories, until they become so far from the truth that sometimes they never know what the truth is."

She grinned and glanced away as she leaned back in her chair. She suddenly had a very faraway look in her eyes. I knew that my mom had a special love for my dad and even though she didn't mention it often, she missed him a lot. As more and more people came west, my dad was spending more and more time away from home. Everyone wanted his help. Everyone thought they needed him - break this horse; lead that cattle drive; fight these Indians; round up this herd; lasso that wild stallion; train these cowboys; catch those robbers. It went on and on. I was not sure if Daniel or Carrie knew much about him at all. And the stories . . . It seemed as the older I got, the wilder and wilder the stories got, as if each retelling had to be more outlandish that the last. Where does the truth end and when does the lie begin? Mom broke the silence of the moment.

"Did you finish all your chores today?"

Just as quickly, she jumped up and started to move around the kitchen with no particular task at hand. She did not wait for an answer.

"Tomorrow is school, and you should be in bed soon. Head on up. I will see you in the morning."

As I passed by her to climb to the loft, she pulled me to her and gave me a very strong hug and a kiss on the top of my head and then went back to piddling in the kitchen. I was tired and I *did* finish my chores. Tomorrow began the last week of school. I was ready. That lazy, easy summer I had hoped to have would be here soon.

CHAPTER 4

THE LAST WEEK OF SCHOOL

My brother, sister and I had just arrived at school as Miss Loganton was ringing the bell. As she stood there, I heard Carrie giggle. When I asked her what was so funny, she answered,

"Miss Loganton is so-o-o skinny. Not like momma!"

I laughed along with her. She was right. Miss Loganton was a lot skinnier than our mother was. It wasn't that our mother was very fat as much as it was that Miss Loganton was very thin. Her whole body looked like it had been stretched tighter than wet cowhide strips on a hot day. Her nose was long and almost pointed. Behind her back, other students would often stick up their noses to mock her. Her dark hair was always pulled taut and twisted in a roll behind her head. I felt this made her look even thinner than she was. No one even knew how old she was. Most men who knew about her couldn't say Miss Loganton was an attractive woman, but they all felt she could have made herself up a little better.

We had not settled in our seats before the talking started up.

"To be the last week of school, it sure don't feel different," said Thomas, seated behind me, whisper loud enough for all of us in the back of the classroom to hear. I heard a collective moan of agreement from all the others. Of course, Thomas complained about everything, but this day he was right.

"Miss Loganton has us doing everything the same as if it was the middle of the year," Silas added. "She is the same every day."

Both boys were the oldest in our school and they were ready to be finished. They had been bragging for months that this was the last year they had to be here. They were both fourteen years old, just about two years older than I was. They were real big for their age, and when they sat on the benches, they looked very awkward with either their long legs stretched out under the front of their desks or their knees hunched to their chests. There was no in between.

Thomas was mean to everyone. He would pick on the little kids before they ever got into the gate. He would check their lunches and if he saw something he liked he would take it and eat it. Everybody knew if you complained he would threaten to beat you up after school. Once you got into the room, it wasn't so bad. The biggest and oldest kids always sat in the back and the smallest and youngest sat in the front, and with Miss Loganton there, everyone felt safe. I guessed I would be on the last row when they were gone next year.

"Just think, I won't have to be around you little brats anymore," boasted Thomas. He had a smirk on his face as he leaned over his desk, and spoke loud enough for only us on the last few rows to hear. "When I'm out of here, I'll have a job soon and I'll be makin' a lot of money. I'm gonna buy the fanciest boots and the biggest hat I can find. Mr. Jacobs told me a body could probably earn ten cents a day working at his general store."

I didn't believe him. Nobody made that much money. I thought to myself, *Ten cents? I'm not sure he could even count that high!* The thought almost made me laugh under my breath. He was terrible with numbers.

Mr. Jacobs always told me how good I was with sums. I remember the first time I went to town and my mom let me pick up our goods at the general store. Mr. Jacobs had started to add up our account.

He had looked at each item we had bought and named off the price of each. "Let's see . . . that's forty-five cents, a dollar twenty-five, ten cents, ten cents, twenty-five cents and twenty cents,"

As he started to add them up, I said, "Two dollars and thirty-five cents."

Mr. Jacobs had looked at me, grinned weakly and continued to add up the total. "Let's see. Carry the one and the total will be . . ." He had paused, stared directly at me and said, "That will be two dollars and thirty-five cents." As he continued to stare, a small smile grew on his face, and then he broke into a big belly laugh.

"Very good, young man. *Very* good," he had said as he finally stopped laughing. He reached in a barrel and pulled out a licorice and handed it to me.

When I remembered that experience, I felt like Mr. Jacobs would not be very impressed with Thomas. He would probably eat all the licorice while Mr. Jacobs was not looking, too.

Not to be outdone, Silas chimed in as well. "I'm goin' buy that fancy black saddle Mr. Ledbetter made and put in the General Store to sell. Just as soon as I find myself a job."

Well, I thought to myself, *it better be a job where he doesn't have to read or write. Even my little sister can read and write better in school than he can!*

I thought neither one of them would be missed. In fact, school would probably be better for everyone once they were gone.

"What's all that talking I am hearing from the back of the room?" snapped Miss Loganton as she spun around from writing on the board.

In the blink of an eye, everyone jerked straight up in their place to face the front with their hands folded on their desktops.

Miss Loganton always wore the same overdress that had a big pocket in the front. In it was a ruler. She would use it to point out something on the board or to draw a straight line, but she would also use it to shake at a student, and sometimes she would pop it across a table or chair and make this loud snapping noise. If ever we got a little rowdy, she would use it. Not to hit the students - just for whacking a table or desk to get our attention. No one had ever seen her hit a student with it, but when you weren't paying attention in class, she could sneak up on you without a sound, and the next thing you heard was this thunderous snap that would almost shoot you off the bench. Everyone thought she was real mean.

When you were new at the school, the older students would tell you how mean she was and by the time you walked into the building, you were scared to death of her.

I remembered my first day when the oldest boys started talking to me and telling me the stories about her.

"She can get it so close to your arm or leg or head when she smacks that ruler on your desk that you think you were shot by a gun, just from the feel of the wind," one of the oldest boys informed me.

Another said, "If she isn't close enough to swing that stick, she can give you a stare that could freeze a creek on a southern slope in the middle of summer."

I was real scared the first few weeks, but then I realized that she was not all that bad. She would smile at you when you did something good, and it made you feel real warm and proud. I was afraid, at first, to say anything in class, but I found out she wanted to hear our questions and answers, as long as we were serious and not trying to be silly in class. If you needed help, she would stand by you and sometimes she would gently touch your shoulder, and you knew she cared.

As we waited for Miss Loganton to finish her writing on the board, Elizabeth Todd raised her hand. When Miss Loganton did not see her right away, Elizabeth began waving it side to side. Soon, her whole body was moving side to side and her motion made the bench squeak; *that* got the teacher's attention.

Miss Loganton turned around and asked, "Yes, Elizabeth?"

"The room is making me hot," she moaned and fluttered her hand in front of her face, trying to create her own breeze.

Elizabeth Todd was *always* hot. No, that was not true. In the winter, she was *always* cold.

"There is not a lot I can do about that, Elizabeth."

"But, Miss Loganton," she whined, "I'm starting to - *perspire!*"

Elizabeth thought she was already a woman. Although Silas and Thomas were the biggest in our school they were not the tallest. Elizabeth was *tall* - taller than any of the boys in our school. Now that I thought about it, she was the tallest girl I had ever seen or remembered. She probably thought this put her in charge of everyone. At least, she would like to think she was in charge. I didn't like her. She was way too bossy. *Much* bossier than Carrie.

In the winter, we had a fire in the pot-bellied stove, and even that did not keep the room warm enough for Elizabeth Todd. The old man who was the keeper at the school came in early on those cold days and started the fire. His name was Mr. Dunbar, and he would cut the wood, split it and stack it outside - enough to last all winter. That in itself was not impressive, but Mr. Dunbar only had one arm. He would do all the work around the school, like repairing the roof, cutting the wood and starting the fire - all with just one arm. People would never ask about what happened to his arm and he never talked about it. He was a very quiet man, and whenever the conversation began to include any comment about him or how he lost his arm, he would just smile and walk on. Of course, everyone had heard many different stories about what happened to him. Once when I was in town near the general store, I overheard several old-timers arguing about Mr. Dunbar.

The first one I heard speak up had just spit out on the street as he leaned back in his chair against the wall of the shop.

"I hear tell he lost it in the War, fightin' with the South." His lips, teeth and the matted beard beneath his chin were stained dark brown from all the tobacco he had chewed for so long. "Some say he lost it at the Battle of Baton Rouge. Shot off by a cannon volley from a Union ship."

"Gawf!" disputed another mangy-bearded man. "I hear'd he was a trapper in the Rockies and had it ripped off by a torturous Grizzly."

"You both are wrong!" asserted the third. "He was in a gun fight where he kilt a man, but not befer he got hisself shot in the arm. Since no doc was around to get the bullet out, he had to cut it off hisself to stop the rot."

The last man who spoke was probably the dirtiest man I had ever seen. Just the smell made me move away from him. I could still hear them arguing even after I had walked across the street.

Whether any of those stories were true or not, Mr. Dunbar would not talk about it. Maybe he thought those stories everyone was telling and hearing was a lot more adventuresome than the truth. The only thing I knew for sure was that he had no family - just himself. He seemed to enjoy being around the students. No one believed he was ever married, so I guessed we were the children he never had. However, no one knew for sure about anything of his life before he drifted into Ringgold.

If the schoolhouse needed any repairs, Mr. Dunbar took care of it. It seemed that in the last few years he had to make more and more repairs. The roof leaked badly last year, and Mr. Dunbar worked a long time to repair it. He had done many things to make the schoolhouse better, but when it got so hot in the early summer like today, he just couldn't do anything to make it any cooler. We were always glad to have the breezes come down the mountains in the spring, but once it got hot in the mountains too, we would never get too many cool winds. I guessed I would agree with Elizabeth. It was very warm today.

Before Miss Loganton could respond, Elizabeth continued to complain.

"Our school house is too old and too hot and too dark and too dirty!"

"Well, Elizabeth, you are right!" Miss Loganton sat on her desk and sighed. "Our school is too old. Do any of you children know the history of this school?" Without waiting for us to answer, she continued.

"It was built long before any of you were born. It started out with one room, but, as more people had continued to move into town, another room was added on. Once there were two teachers, but they both got married and moved away. When I was invited to teach here, I was asked if I could handle all the students together. They had such a hard time finding one teacher, they felt they could never find two. And, I was so anxious to get a job, I said 'Yes, I could.', and here I am. We don't need two rooms anymore. It would be nice to have another teacher and divide our class between the older students and the younger ones, but so far, I am all you have. Having a new school . . . well, it is hard to ask the town to build a new school when we are using only half of this one."

I was surprised to hear that story. I never knew the other room was a classroom. The only thing I ever saw it used for was for storing firewood and broken desks and benches. A school with more than one teacher? What a strange school that would be!

Miss Loganton took a deep breath and fanned her face with her hand. "Yes, it is too hot in here, but we have no control over the weather. And I know as soon as I tell you it is time for recess, you will all run out to the yard and no one will be complaining about the weather then. Am I right? Unless, of course, you would prefer to stay inside and out of the sun's heat."

She looked around the room, and she knew we dared not say anything that would cause us not to have recess.

"And yes, Elizabeth, it is too dark in here. But, if we open the windows even wider for more light, we just let more dust in and then it will be even dirtier in here." She stood up from her desk and walked to her place in the middle of the classroom. "Now," she continued as she looked around at all the students, "I am sure we can open the windows even more. But, I will need a few volunteers to stay with me after school every day to clean up the extra dirt. I'm sure I can find a few rags and extra brooms and we can stay to make sure the floors and desks and benches and rafters and walls are as clean as Miss Elizabeth wishes they were."

Miss Loganton glanced around the room but no one volunteered. She added, "Well, I guess things must stay as they are. With that, it is time to continue our work."

I never realized it before, but, except for the Turnipseeds, not many new people moved here anymore, and many had moved away.

As I looked around, I noticed that everything in the room was a brownish-gray color - the walls, the floors, the desks and chairs, even the rafters that held up the roof. It was true, our school was old. The windows had shutters for when it got too cold or too windy or rainy; otherwise they were open and the little sunlight that came through made the room look a little bit brighter. The floor was hard and you always made a lot of noise when you walked on it. Miss Loganton always knew if you were moving around in your seat - she could hear the smallest creak and squeak in those floorboards. Some days, if we were real fidgety, the noise would make Miss Loganton almost pull her hair out.

We had two large pictures of George Washington and Abraham Lincoln on the wall and an American flag was draped over a flagpole in the corner. Miss Loganton had a very old desk with a huge top. She always kept it clean, and she had her books standing neatly on the corner. When she sat down behind it, she looked so tiny; like a toothpick peering over the side of a barrel. Of course, she did not sit behind it often. She was either writing on the blackboard, or explaining a lesson or walking around the room, checking our work.

Every day, she would sit on a small stool in the back of the room when we read to her and when she read to us. We would all sit around her on the floor. Once we had settled down and got real quiet for her to read, it seemed the day would cool off a little. Sometimes it was hard not to take to napping; especially when a welcome breeze would pick up and blow through the open windows and cracks in the walls. This was probably our favorite time at school, aside from recess. Except for numbers, I knew it was *my* favorite time. Miss Loganton had a special way of reading. It made us feel like we were right there with all those characters that she would read about.

Everyone became real antsy as the week wore on, but she didn't let us rest or have a break or have any fun. Miss Loganton said fun is for recess. I knew that when you have a busy day at school it was supposed to go faster, but this day seemed very slow. When we were studying sums, it was like free time for me. I could usually just think about my horses. I would especially be thinking about my great white stallion. I would often dream about riding him through town or leading a cattle drive or chasing bank robbers across the plains. But this day I was not thinking about horses. As I looked around my class, I wondered if anyone here knew that the Turnipseeds had a daughter named Samantha. I wondered why she did not come to school. Mom said she was smart. *Was she so smart that she didn't need school?* I thought to myself. *I'm very smart and my mom says I still have more schoolin' ahead.* She couldn't be that much smarter than me. *Was she so special that she was too good to go with us?* Well, I have seen her younger brother and sisters - Robert, Rachel and Maggie - at school almost every day. *They* came to school here.

"Billy!" Miss Loganton had interrupted my thoughts. "Just because you think you know ciphering does not mean you can sit and day dream," she scolded. "Could you please explain to the class how to solve this problem?"

I jumped to my feet, but I thought, *What problem? I wasn't listening enough to know what she was talking about.* I paused ever so briefly before I confessed, "I-I'm sorry, Miss Loganton, I -I don't know."

With that, the class burst out laughing at me. I could hear several indistinct voices mocking me, and I was sure my face was beet red. Miss Loganton admonished the class for their outburst, and called on another student, but it was too late. I was so embarrassed!

I slowly settled back into my seat, and I lowered my head. If they knew I was thinking about a girl, they would have *really* been teasing me, and I would be in real trouble – not with the teacher, but the other boy students. I decided to ask Maggie or Robert or Rachel about their sister. No - just Robert would be better. He was a boy. Girls would just tattle. He would tell me why Samantha did not come to school.

I needed to know now!

CHAPTER 5

WHO WAS SAMANTHA TURNIPSEED?

It was recess, and I had decided to ask Robert about his sister. I felt funny going on the side where the younger children played. It was an unspoken rule that the older students never played with the younger ones, and the younger ones better not come on our side. Any big boy caught on the other side of the school yard was considered a sissy, unless, of course, you went with a group to boss around the little ones. Then it was OK. Sometimes the girls in my class went on that side, but they would go and teach the little ones how to play games. But the boys? Not by themselves. Never!

I was standing on the edge - still on my side but close enough to the other side to see the little children, and maybe even talk to them without anyone noticing. I tried to kick a few rocks around the yard and then I glanced up to see if anyone was watching me. I kicked a rock closer and closer to the big tree near where Robert was playing tag with some of the other boys his age. I dared not go near the girls. I would be branded a sissy for sure. Without being too close, I muttered to Robert as he quickly ran past,

"Where's your sister?"

He barely paused, but uttered, "They're both playing by the fence," as he motioned with his head and continued running.

Not those sisters, I said to myself. I continued watching to make sure the older boys couldn't see me as I waited for Robert to draw near me again.

As he did, I whispered again,

"I mean Samantha," and, without breaking his stride, he yelled back matter-of-factly,

"Home."

I thought, *I must not be asking the right question*, and recess was almost over. I was beginning to get frustrated and I started to call Robert, but he was too far away. This time I ran over and grabbed him. I held on to his shoulders, looked him in the eye and very clearly and deliberately slow I said,

"Why don't she come to school?" He looked puzzled that anyone would be so curious about his sister. Suddenly Miss Loganton began to ring the bell that recess was over. As I glanced back toward the school, Robert tore himself away from me and as he was running back to the building, he yelled out,

"She has her own teacher."

Her own teacher? One teacher just for her? Well, maybe she is too special for the rest of us. Maybe her parents think she is too good for the rest of us... Maybe her parents think she is too smart to come to our little school.

By now, I was the last one in the building. As I walked into the class, I felt many eyes following me to my seat. As Miss Loganton quieted the class, I looked up to see other students giggling and pointing at me. As I looked at each one, they would snicker and hide their faces. *What was going on? What did I do? Why was everyone laughing and staring at me?* I felt my face begin to flush and I knew it was red again. I could feel the palms of my hands sweating. When Miss Loganton turned to write our work on the board, I heard a voice behind me call out enough for me to hear but not for Miss Loganton,

"Billy, have fun with the babies?" It sounded just like Thomas.

"Only sissies play with the babies." This voice was Silas, I knew.

"Baby Billy, Baby Billy . . ."

Soon, several picked up the chant and it became so loud I couldn't believe Miss Loganton did not hear it. When she quickly turned around, all the noise suddenly stopped, but I could still hear an occasional giggle and snicker. I was embarrassed, again. I didn't think anyone could see me. I was so careful. Now everyone thought I was a sissy, just because I asked one question on the littluns' side. It was a question about a girl I didn't even know, and twice already she had caused me trouble. I needed to forget about this girl . . . . could I?

CHAPTER 6

SCHOOL WAS OUT

I thought the last week of school would never end. I tried to keep my mind on getting my work done, but sometimes it was not easy. By this time of the year my dad would have been back home already, and then would have headed out with the herd. It seemed I had not seen him in such a long time. Another reason was the teasing I got all week. I was real embarrassed at first, but soon all the giggling and laughing slowly ended - except for Thomas and Silas. They never forgot anything, and brought it up every time they saw me.

I tried not to think about Samantha much, and I dared not try to talk to any of her brothers or sister again when other boys were around. Now that school was almost out, I was not sure how I could find out more about her. I surely would not ask my mom because I did not want her to tease me about it either. And my little brother and sister? If I said something to them, they would tell everyone and act like I was courtin' and sparkin' her or something. That would be embarrassing. I was only glad no one knew what I was asking Robert. Then I thought about church. Maybe I could find out something about her at church.

The first few days after school had ended, I spend a lot of fun time with my horses. I did not see many of my friends from school. Everyone was busy for a reason – either to help their families around their farms and ranches or hired on already to a heard headed for the trail. Every year in the past, my dad would have been home by now and gone, taking our herd to market. I had been watching the cattle and I took them regularly to different pasture lands to graze. We did not have a lot of cattle, but we needed more land to graze them than we owned. My dad had bartered with our neighbors to use some of their land to pasture our cattle. I could tell they were getting fat. They should bring a good price at the yards. My dad always had the best cattle. He could take a scrawny old heifer, and by the time he got her to market, he would have her grown into a prize piece of cattle. When he went to market, we always got top dollar. Dad should have been here by now.

The days seemed to be getting longer and hotter. West Texas summers could be harsh. It seemed like everyone was getting a late start. By now, all the local ranchers had already brought their herds in and they had headed them east, then north, along a trail that my dad helped start years ago. Usually getting there first got you the best price.

I never actually went on a trail ride with my dad. I would ride with him and spend the day out on the trail, but as soon as we finished supper, my dad would send me back. I was never more than a day away from home; at most, 10 or 12 miles, since that was about what a cattle drive could cover in a day. When I knew he was coming in, my mom would let me go out to meet him. But this summer he was the latest he had ever been. If we didn't get them to market we would lose money, and it would make the winter hard for us. School would be starting in a few months, and I had hoped this year to stay with him longer than just a day's ride away. Usually someone came through town and let the rest of us know who was coming in and when, and other news from along the trail. But this year there was no word, at least about my dad. I didn't ask anyone about him. I knew my dad must still be gone for a reason. He wouldn't just not come home unless it was important. I knew he would be here soon.

"Billy! Bil-l-l-l-y! Hook up the wagon! You need to go to town!" I heard Mom call from the porch all the way to the stable. I was already on Whiskers. Sometimes I rode him around the fields just to make him move. He was so slow and acted so old. He walked as slow as an old man - never in a hurry. It didn't take long to get him hitched and ready. As Mom walked out to meet me, she reached up to give me a list and said,

"Go to Mr. Jacobs' General Store. I saw him in church on Sunday and he is expecting you. I was hoping your dad would be here by now, but I can't wait for him to get our supplies."

This was the first time Mom mentioned Dad being late. We both knew this was the longest he had ever stayed away. For the first time, I saw a worried look on her face.

I was soon on the road and, before long, I arrived in town. Our town was very small. Its name was Ringgold. I never knew why. We had no gold and I'm not sure what the "ring" part meant. We had a livery stable and a leather shop - side-by-side and owned by Mr. Ledbetter. He was a burly man with huge hands and his hair had either all fallen out or else he shaved his head all the time. Even though he could pound away on horseshoes all day, he could also sit and make the most beautiful leather saddles and bridles. He even made boots, if a person didn't need them for a long time.

We had no hotel like I'd heard some other towns had. We did have a Sheriff's office, but it was small and the jail was rarely used. In fact, except for some occasional town drunks, it had never been used much. I don't remember us having any real outlaws. Since our town did not have a saloon, you couldn't buy liquor, so there weren't many in town who got drunk. Of course there were always outsiders who staggered into town and would end up in our jail.

Now we had a bank that the Turnipseed family built. We also had a barbershop and Mr. Meeks was the owner. Mr. Meeks was a very tall man with big teeth. His hair was short and always parted on one side. He had it combed over and oiled flat to his head. I guessed a barber needed to have nice hair. Of course, I never had him cut my hair. My mom did that. I'm glad she didn't slick my hair down like Mr. Meeks. I wouldn't like it. But Mr. Meeks did more than just give shaves and cut hair. A person could get a hot bath there, too. Often travelers passing through on their way from and to California came for a bath and they'd wash their clothes and hang them out to dry behind the shop while they bathed. And, if a person had a bad tooth that ached, Mr. Meeks was known to pull teeth a time or two.

Other than the bank, livery stable and leather shop, barbershop, jail and the General Store, Ringgold did not have many other stores in town. At least, not now.

There was the tobacco shop that wasn't open since all the trail riders were gone. Mr. Horton sold pipes and tobacco and he had these little machines that would roll cigars and cigarettes. The men folk would buy the pipes and cigars, but they preferred buying the paper and pouches of tobacco to roll their own cigarettes.

The cooper was Mr. Hans Anderson. He was only here for a few weeks at a time, and then he would move from town to town, making barrels, buckets, butter churns, tubs and anything else a farmer or rancher might need, like crates or bins. He had a whole collection of utensils he would shape out of wood and sell in the General Store. He was also good at making pipes. He would make them out of corncobs as well as out of fancy wood with carved faces of animals and people for the bowl, and Mr. Horton would sell them in his shop.

Another store was run by Mr. and Mrs. Solomon just at the edge of town.

They made hats. Mrs. Solomon was the milliner who made hats for the ladies and Mr. Solomon was the hatter who made them for the men. They would work together; when you saw one, you saw the other. They were always together. The Solomons did not go to our church. I was told they were Jewish which meant they closed every Saturday. They never mingled with the other people in the town, but they always had lots of business from the men and the women who wanted to buy their hats. Everyone said their hats were the best made anywhere around West Texas. My dad always bought our hats from them, but my mom always preferred her bonnets.

A few weeks earlier, the town was full of cattle being held in corrals just on the edge of town. Farmers and ranchers all around the panhandle would bring their smaller herds to be sold to the trail bosses who had gathered in town to do some buying. But now that the cattle had all been taken on the trail, the feed lot, the tanner shop and the agent office were all closed down until the next year when it was time to start the trail ride again. Very few families actually had houses in town. Most folk lived just outside of town on the ranches or farmhouses that spread out all around Ringgold.

Mr. Jacobs owned the General Store and it was the most popular place around. Of course, the barbershop was popular, but only with the men folk. Sometimes travelers or outsiders would stop in for a rest and to share news of what was happening here and what was happening everywhere else. The women folk never went there. One reason was that women hardly ever cut their hair, and the other was that when they needed their hair cut, they'd cut each other's. I remembered my mom cutting the neighbors' hair before. Anyway, they never had a barbershop for women folk to go to.

If a person was expecting mail or needed to send a letter, the General Store was the place to go. Mr. Jacobs served as our postmaster and his store was our post office.

As I walked into Mr. Jacobs' store, I thought about what a very funny looking man he was. I liked him. He was strangely round with very skinny legs. His nose was big and his hands were hard and stubby. A pencil was always tucked behind his ear. He was always smiling, and when he opened his mouth, you saw this dark mark on his tongue where he would lick his pencil every time before he wrote. I liked him because I could count on a licorice every time we bought at his store. This day he was much busier than normal. His store seemed full of people. Everybody came to the General Store. Mr. Jacobs saw me and nodded his head to acknowledge my presence, and I placed my list on the counter. I liked his store too, especially his saddles, bridles and boots he would sell for Mr. Ledbetter. I saw the beautiful black saddle that Silas often talked about. I could close my eyes and see that very saddle strapped to the white stallion. As I leaned near it, I could smell the strong, fresh scent of leather. I liked walking around. He had a new shipment of planks stacked near the back door and I sucked in the strong woody smell. I then passed the bolts of fabrics with their bright colors, and as I brushed my hands across the soft textures and felt the smooth touch of the material, I heard a familiar voice.

"Master William! Is that you?" I jerked around and it was exactly who I thought - Mrs. Turnipseed. She didn't wait for a response. "My! My! It is! How are you young man?" She continued before I could answer. "My Samantha was just asking about you again this morning."

Samantha? I said to myself. *Asking about me? What do you mean again?* I had forgotten how much I disliked the Turnipseeds, but for this one brief moment I didn't care because I wanted her to tell me more about Samantha.

"Did your mother not give you the message?"

What message? I asked myself. *About what?*

"I tried to speak with you at church on an occasion these last several weeks or so, but you were always out and about, and I never could catch you."

Now she paused, and her eye caught a particular pattern sitting on the shelf.

I looked intently at her. *What message?* I screamed in my head.

"You know," she continued, as she pulled a colorful bolt of material off the shelf, and ran her hand across it, "this would make a lovely apron." She leaned down towards me as if to whisper some grand secret, and said, "I usually have to order all my fabrics direct from the East. Unless of course I can find one of those store-bought dresses from the catalogs Mr. Jacobs gets every few months. In fact, I ordered one last month and it should be arriving soon. I need to speak to Mr. Jacobs about that." She glanced up as if to look for Mr. Jacobs.

What does that have to do with the message? I was becoming impatient, but she was now intently looking over *all* the bolts of material on Mr. Jacobs' shelves and was still talking about her dresses. I was not hearing a word and I couldn't keep being polite.

I blurted out, "Mrs. Turnipseed, what message?"

"Hum? Oh, yes, Samantha had asked if you could visit one Sunday afternoon."

Samantha wanted me to visit? How long ago did she ask? When did you ask my mom? A hundred questions raced through my mind, but I uttered none of them.

For once, Mrs. Turnipseed paused to hear a response from me.

All I could do was smile and nod.

"Well then," she broke the silence, "I take that as a 'yes'. We will be happy to have you, say, around 3 o'clock this Sunday, perhaps?"

I nodded in agreement, and she was gone in a moment. I could hear her talking to Mr. Jacobs and soon the store was unusually quiet. Mr. Jacobs shouted at me,

"Billy! I have all your goods ready for loading."

I turned around and headed for the counter. Everything was stacked and ready, and I began to grab the items and move slowly to the door, my arms full of flour, salt, and oats. After three more trips back and forth, I was done. My mind was still on the conversation I had with Mrs. Turnipseed. Once I grabbed the reins, Whiskers knew what to do. I rode home with my mind full of questions and my stomach full of butterflies. *Sunday? That was tomorrow! What would I say? What would we talk about? Should I dress up? Would we go outside? Would we stay inside? Would her parents be with us?* It wasn't until tomorrow and I was already very nervous.

Once home, I unhooked Whiskers and put away the wagon. I had unloaded the goods to the back porch, and Mom, Daniel and Carrie started bringing everything into the house. I could hear lots of talking, but I wasn't listening. I was still thinking about tomorrow. Once I got into the house, supper was almost ready. Carrie was setting the table, and I watched her place every plate and spoon in perfect alignment. She was so intent on her job at hand that she did not notice me watching her. She looked just like I imagined my mom looked when she was Carrie's age. My chubby, round-faced little sister with her little stubby fingers could hardly hold the plates and I was sure she would drop one on the floor. As I watched her, I could see she was trying to be so careful and not drop anything. Her long dress made her look taller than she was. She was just as friendly as Mom; always eager to laugh, and never shy. She was different from Daniel. He was the shy one. Often it was Carrie who helped Daniel meet new friends, even though there were almost three years between them. If it weren't for Carrie, Daniel would be playing by himself all the time. She had always liked being around people and she was a good sister to Daniel and always wanted him to play. He was good-hearted and put up with his sister's outgoingness.

"Very nice, Carrie," Mom said, interrupting my thoughts, "You did a wonderful job!"

Carrie looked up, and they both beamed at each other. While I was deep in thought about my sister and brother, the table had been set with food and Daniel had joined us. As soon as we are seated, we instinctually reached to hold the hand of the one next to us around the table. Mom was at one end with Carrie and Daniel on either side. I sat next to Daniel with an empty chair for Dad at the other end. We bowed our heads and Mom prayed,

"Oh, Lord, we thank You for Your blessings on our home and family. We thank You for the food You provide for us. We pray for Bill. Watch over him and protect him from harm. In Your Name, we ask. Amen."

As we began to eat, I noticed my mom's face. I didn't remember her looking this sad before. She did not look me in the eye. Maybe she didn't want to talk. It was a quiet meal and, once we had finished, everyone helped clear the table and wash, dry, and put away the dishes. There was a little small talk about the chickens Daniel and Carrie had to catch when they escaped the coop and about the weather, but no mention of Dad. I knew Mom was worried. For a moment, I had forgotten about my visit to the Turnipseeds on Sunday. Soon Daniel and Carrie were off to bed. I was allowed to stay up longer since I was the oldest. There seemed to be so much to talk about with my mom, but nothing was coming out. I sat at the table with a candle before me and I played with the lit wick. Its brightness was coating the room with flashing waves of lights as I made it flicker. Suddenly my mom appeared at my side with a strange look on her face, and said,

"Billy, I almost forgot. I talked to Mrs. Turnipseed at church last week. Or was it the week before? No, maybe before that. . ." She was trying to recall the exact day and she had this puzzled look on her face.

"I know Mom, I saw her today at Mr. Jacobs' store. She invited me over tomorrow in the afternoon." I did not mention Samantha's name.

"I'm sorry I forgot to tell you. With things as they are right now . . . " Her voice trailed off and she moved away from the table. I was sure she was thinking about my dad. I told her good night and as I moved to climb the ladder to the loft, I thought I could hear her sobbing ever so softly. I knew she did not want me to hear her, so I climbed quickly to the loft and quietly slipped into my bed. I lay there for a moment. My final thought of the day was not about my horses or even the great white one; nor was it about my meeting with Samantha tomorrow; it was how much I missed my dad.

CHAPTER 7

SUNDAY AROUND OUR TABLE

That Sunday we were at church early, and Carrie and Daniel were off and running. I was usually not far behind them. But that Sunday I was watching for the Turnipseeds. I stayed in the wagon and I kept a constant vigil for their buggy. When I saw it coming, I tried to see if Samantha was with them. She was not. *Why doesn't she come to church?* Robert and Rachel were with their parents. I soon saw another buggy. It was Charles and Clark and someone else. My heart leaped, but then I realized it was just Maggie. Counting Samantha, there were six children in the Turnipseed family. Only Samantha did not come to church. *Who stayed with her?* I guessed Britt did.

Church seemed extra-long that day, and Mom wanted to stay extra-long to chat and laugh. It was not any longer than normal, but it just felt that way.

It did not matter where I was, I wanted to get to the next thing. I wanted church to start. As soon as it started, I wanted it to end. When it ended, I wanted to go home. When I got home, I wanted it to be time to go to the Turnipseeds. I felt so jumpy. I believe my mom noticed it, too. At the dinner table, she began to talk about Dad, and she seemed cheerier. She said a letter had arrived for her after I left Mr. Jacobs yesterday. She said it might be from Dad. I hoped so.

"Mrs. Jacobs told me that Mr. Jacobs would be at the store today because a big delivery was supposed to arrive," Mom said. "He will be there late this afternoon and he would gladly wait for you."

It seemed to cheer Mom up. As we sat around the table, we all began to relax. Mom was in a better mood, and we all sensed it and it made the noon meal more enjoyable. We laughed as Daniel told a story about one of his friends falling asleep in church.

"Daniel, was he really asleep?" Mom prodded Daniel to tell more about his story.

"Yes Mommy, he was," explained Daniel. "His head kept flopping side to side."

Daniel demonstrated by moving his head in exaggerated fashion as he swung his body from one side to the other, almost falling off his chair.

"Thad was using the big Bible off the table in the front of the church, and then he fell asleep on the front row. When the pastor told us to open our Bibles, I nudged him with my elbow," Daniel demonstrated and he continued, "He woke up and when he saw everyone staring at him, he threw open the Bible and started reading the first thing he saw!"

This gave Carrie the giggles, and that made all of us laugh even longer and harder. Before I knew it, it was almost 3 o'clock. As the laughter quieted down, we all helped clear the table, and Daniel and Carrie scooted outdoors. Mom sat down and took a deep breath.

"Well, Master William," she said, mocking Mrs. Turnipseed, "I'm so charmed you dined with us today."

With that we both broke out in roars of laughter again. With tears in our eyes from the laughing, Mom sighed and reminded me about my appointment at the Turnipseeds. She looked at me real serious like and said,

"I can't imagine you'd want to go there again." Then she cocked her head and said, "It couldn't be that pretty little golden-haired girl, Samantha, could it?"

"Mom!" I moaned. She smiled and grabbed my hand.

"Billy, you're growing up. It's all right. You are a very handsome fella. You are a lot like your dad. Daniel looks like him, too, but you have those wonderful eyes like him and that dark black head of hair. I couldn't resist your dad's eyes, and no girl will be able to resist yours either," she smiled.

Now my heart was really racing. I *was* growing up. I *was* already thirteen. I *was* the man in charge here when Dad was gone. *But why was I so nervous?* I couldn't tell my mom. Maybe one day I would ask her about how I was feeling right now. Now? I had to go to Samantha's.

I told my mom goodbye, and I started out the door.

"Billy," she called, "Don't forget to get that letter from Mr. Jacobs this afternoon. He'll be waiting for you at his store."

"I won't forget. I promise."

"Bye," she called out as she waved and watched me leave.

I was already on Darlin' and half way out the gate when I yelled back, "Bye."

All of a sudden, my stomach knotted up and I asked myself, *What am I doing?*

CHAPTER 8

I FINALLY TALKED WITH SAMANTHA

Sitting around the table and having dinner with my family had made me feel a little more comfortable and at ease, and my mom gave me some confidence as I headed for the Turnipseeds. But the closer I got, the more uncertain I became. All the same questions kept coming back. *What was I going to say? What were we going to talk about? Was I dressed good enough?* I had been rushing all day and as I rode down the road I began to think about how I acted the last time I was here. I began to feel embarrassed about it. I thought about the Turnipseeds. They were so rich. They had so much. They talked different. They made me wash outside and use the rear entrance. I had already gotten in trouble twice at school because I was thinking about Samantha.

I began to slow Darlin's pace, almost to a stop. *Did I really want to do this? Why did she want to see me?* I had been past her house several times over the summer. I thought about when I met her. It was two weeks before the end of school. It had already been almost a month since then. I would always watch for her, but I never saw her; always her brothers and sisters, but never her. She never came outside.

I liked being out. I enjoyed riding. One day I would have a horse as grand and as smart and wonderful as my dad's. I loved Princess and Darlin' and even Whiskers, but I wanted him. I had seen him on the Bluffs and running near Devil's Pass. He was a wild one but he was the only one I wanted. Horses were my life and would be forever. I had to be outside. Without even noticing, I had ridden up to the Turnipseeds house.

"You're William, aren't you?" My daydream was broken by the voice of Charles or Clark. I didn't know one from the other. He had come down from the porch steps of the house to greet me.

"Y-yes," I stuttered.

"I'm Charles. You remember me, don't you, from dinner quite a few weeks ago?"

"Yes," I lied. I remembered he was at the table, but I didn't remember if he was Charles or Clark.

"Welcome. My little sister is waiting for you. We're glad you could come."

I dismounted, and he took Darlin' and, as he led me up to the house, he leaned over and whispered in my ear,

"She has talked of nothing but you since the day you were here. But don't you ever mention it. It would embarrass her completely. Just between us men folk, right?"

I nodded in agreement, amazed that he considered me part of the "men folk" and shocked about his sister. I couldn't say a word.

"Come. Sit on the veranda. I will fetch her," he said. "Would you care for a refreshment?"

I nodded again, still in shock. *She had been thinking of me? Ever since that day at her house?* He handed my horse off to a farm hand, and Charles disappeared into the house. I slowly moved to a large swing near the front door. I could hear voices coming from the house. I recognized Robert's voice. In a flash, the front door flew open as Robert, his twin Rachel and Maggie all raced out the door and stood expectantly in front of me. There they stood, hands held behind their backs, bright, wide smiles on their faces, staring directly at me. I tried to ignore them, but they continued to stare.

Then Mrs. Turnipseed came out and said, "Scoot! Scoot! Master William is not here to see you! Go play!"

They did not move.

"Now!" she admonished, and she stamped her foot hard on the wooden porch floor. At that, they scurried off into the yard.

"So delighted you could come," she continued. "Did Charles offer you refreshment?" Before I could answer, Britt had swung the door open and was bringing out a large tray of small cakes and lemonade with two small glasses.

"Oh, here it is. Set it on the table here, Britt, and could you please get Samantha? Her friend is here." Britt did not say a word. She knew, like I did, that Mrs. Turnipseed did not expect an answer. Britt paused as she looked at me with the widest smile I had ever seen on a person's face. As Mrs. Turnipseed started back into the house, Britt hesitated and then whispered to me,

"Samantha does not have many friends. I do hope you will be one." It was a very serious tone in her voice, almost like begging.

Then the tone changed to a more cheerful one and she said, "I will leave you two alone to talk about whatever two young people talk about."

Before she left, Britt poured a glass of lemonade. I guessed it was for me. It was on my side of the tray. The other glass was so far away. I figured Samantha's mom did not want her sitting next to me. Just as I went to grab my glass, the front door swung open. It startled me so much that I knocked the glass off the tray, and lemonade splashed all over the table. As the glass started to roll off the table, I tried to reach and catch it. Instead I slipped out of the swing, falling face down on the hard surface as the glass came crashing to the floor, breaking into a hundred pieces. As I tried to quickly recover, I raised myself up, only to have the swing hit me in the back of the head as it swung forward. I fell forward again and now lay motionless on the porch. I could see pieces of glass everywhere. I felt the coolness of the lemonade as my clothes soaked it up. The back of my head really hurt! I felt as if I could have crawled into a hole and died!

As I lay there, I heard an eruption of laughter. I slowly turned my head and looked up to see Samantha seated right before me with Britt at her side, both laughing uncontrollably. Other members of the family soon joined them. Charles was now there with Mrs. Turnipseed, and the three younger children were back on the porch. All were laughing and pointing and talking loudly as I laid in a pool of lemonade with shards of glass all around me. My head was hurting, my clothes were soaked, and I was so embarrassed! I heard Mrs. Turnipseed's voice.

"Help him up, Charles. Britt, let's get the broom and pick up this glass. Children, off the porch! Get back to your play."

Charles lifted me up, avoiding the glass, which was everywhere. He helped me back to the swing, as I collapsed and leaned back in it. I couldn't even raise my eyes to those still there.

"Charles," Mrs. Turnipseed barked, "Don't we have some old clothes Master

William can change into?" Without waiting for a reply, she said, "Take him upstairs and find him some dry clothes."

Charles took my arm and led me quickly into the house.

"Check his head, Charles. If it hurts, I have a tonic," called out Mrs. Turnipseed. My eyes were almost closed as I winced in pain, or what I thought was pain. Maybe it was just the embarrassment. I just followed along as Charles led me up the stairs.

"Well, young fellow, what an impression you have made on my sister," he said as we entered a room full of large trunks and boxes.

I glanced up with a rather disgusted look on my face as Charles tried to console me.

"Don't worry. Years from now, you will be laughing about this episode yourself." He rummaged through several large trunks. "Here are some breeches and an old shirt of Clark's. He won't mind. I think anything I have will be too big on you. Come on downstairs when you finish." He stopped at the door and said, "Oh, by the way, how's your head?"

I rubbed the back of my head, and I couldn't feel any pain. "I'm fine," I answered.

With that, he was out of the room and the door was closed. The clothes fitted me better than I thought they would. There was a large mirror in the room. I looked at myself and I could see me from head to toe. I wondered how my dad looked at my age. I wondered if he had ever done anything as foolish as I had just now. I was almost too embarrassed to go back downstairs. I was not even sure I could find my way. I opened the door and looked around. This was the biggest house I have ever been in. There were large stairs as the end of the hall.

As I turned to go down, I could see Charles at the foot. He looked up and said, "Well done! You look fine! Clark's clothes look better on you than on him. Come on down. We're all waiting."

Great, I thought to myself. *I have to face them all again. What are they waiting for? To laugh at me one more time?* Charles walked out the door ahead of me, and I followed behind. I could see the porch was clean and dry, and the tray had a new glass of lemonade for me. I saw the back of Samantha's chair. It was tall and stiff looking. It had large wheels on each side. As I moved around her, I could see smaller wheels in the front. She looked very tiny sitting there. I could not look at her directly at first. I carefully sat back down on the swing. In a flash, all the others were gone, and there was no one else around except the two of us.

What seemed like an eternity of silence was broken when I heard Samantha say, "You are very funny! I haven't laughed that hard in a long time!"

I could hear her begin to chuckle, and I slowly raised my eyes to see her. I could not help myself, and, I too, began to grin, and soon we were both laughing so hard we couldn't control it. Neither could talk as we laughed and mimicked the event that had just happened. It was several minutes before we finally caught our breath, and each of us gave a big sigh. With smiles still on our faces, Samantha began to tell me,

"I am so glad you came today. I have been waiting several weeks to really meet you." She paused, and her tone became more serious. "You left so suddenly when you were here for dinner with your family. I have heard so many things about your dad. My mother and father asked too many questions. I guess you did not want to hear all that did you?"

She was right. *Was that the real reason I left?* I didn't know. I just get tired of hearing so many questions about my dad sometimes. I hoped she was not like that. She continued without a comment from me.

"I know what it's like. I've gotten questions about my dad all the time. People can ask the dumbest questions, like 'How much money does your father have?'" She had put her hands on her hips and moved her shoulders up and down a she spoke in a very prissy voice, "Or 'How rich *are* you?' or 'Does *all* the money in the bank belong to you?' People are dumb, huh?"

She started laughing and I joined her. It was nice that someone understood. I didn't tell her all the dumb questions people asked me. I was now looking at her face. I didn't think I had ever seen such beautiful eyes. They were so blue. Her skin was so pale and smooth. She leaned back, and a soft smile appeared on her face.

"I've seen you pass my house in the past several weeks," she said, "but you never stop."

"You did? You do? I mean - you saw me? When?" I wanted to say I looked for her every time I passed, but I wasn't sure what she would think.

"Yes, many times. I can see you from my window, right next to the porch. I sit there and read and sew and watch the world, and I have seen you pass on your horse many times." *Many times?* I didn't realize I had passed here many times. I'd made trips to town to get supplies at the General Store, once to the leather shop for a bridle and then the blacksmith for shoeing, but many? I didn't recollect more.

She glanced around, as if looking for something.

"Where is your light brown mare or are you on the little one with the long mane, or that slow pokey one? What is his name, Whiskers?"

How did she know my horses? I knew I had ridden all three at one time or another past her house, but how would she have known their names?

"I'm on Darlin', the light brown one," I replied, still in amazement that she knew my horses, "Your brother Charles had him brought around back."

"She is pretty. But, I had a horse once that looked a lot like Princess."

Her face at that moment became very still, and her voice began to fade, and her eyes were looking very far away. She was lost in thought and I began to really study her. For the first time, I looked down at her legs. They were covered by a long flowing dress and they seemed much too thin for her body. She had very tiny shoes on with large buckles on the sides. They were white and looked as if they were brand new. She broke the pensive mood and turned only to see me staring at her feet. I snapped straight up as she leaned towards me and in a playful, deep voice she comically whispered,

"They don't work too well." She had wrinkled her nose and pursed her lips, but then began to smile. At first, I was embarrassed, but her humor put me at ease. I repeated her statement,

"They don't work too well? Wh- What do you mean?"

"The horse I told you about that was a lot like Princess? She was beautiful. Her name was Olivia. I named her after my great-grandmother. She was a dark brown, almost like a chocolate," she paused as if to wait for my reaction.

"And," I encouraged, hoping she would get to the point.

"Well, I was riding her a few years back, and she hit a rock and fell." She stopped and continued to look at my face as if she was trying to study it. I was becoming a little conscious of her stare, so I asked impatiently,

"What happened?"

"Well," she replied as she leaned back in her chair, and grabbed a strand of her long blond hair and began to twirl it in her fingers, "There was bad news and there was good news."

She knew she was holding me in suspense. I could sense she was playing with me. I was now leaning toward her, holding onto each word. *She was doing this on purpose, I thought, trying to grab my attention, trying to see how I would act.* This was probably a story she has told many times and now she had learned how to keep her listeners on the edge of their seats. I wanted to hear the story, but I was not going to act like a fool. I waited for her to continue. I imagine she saw the look of impatience on my face, and she soon dropped her hair and crossed her hands in her lap.

"Well," she continued in a more serious tone, "The bad news is they had to shoot Olivia."

She paused again and stared directly at me.

And the good news? I thought to myself. *What is the good news?*

She was enjoying my reaction; how she had captivated my attention, how I was listening so intently, how I was eagerly trying to pull every word out of her. I could not resist, and I exploded in a loud voice,

"And the good news?" I felt my ears flushing red and my eyes widening as if to hear and picture the story better in my head.

"The good news is - they didn't shoot *me*." She leaned back and started laughing at the utter blankness of my face.

Shoot you? I didn't get it. *Let me see if I understand.* I repeated in my head what I just heard. *They had to shoot your horse, but the good news is they did not shoot you.*

I slowly leaned back on the swing and I shook my head, not really understanding what she meant. She sensed my confusion and then began to explain,

"Don't you understand, Olivia broke her leg - bad- and they had to shoot her. I was so sad, I cried for days, for weeks, even months."

"I understand that. I know horses. I've seen it happen before. It happened to one of mine. But, but," I was stuttering, trying to see what was so funny about them not shooting her.

"Don't you see?" It was as if she was pleading with me to understand. She leaned as close to me as she could. Her eyes were soft and she had grasped her hands together as if in prayer. "Something happened to my legs too. When I fell off Olivia, I broke something in my back and my legs didn't work either, but they didn't shoot me!"

Now, again, she smiled and slowly leaned back in her chair. Her face changed and a very serious tone was now set in her voice.

"I can't walk, Billy. I'm paralyzed. I will never walk again. I will never ride again. I will never have a horse again. That is why you don't see me at school. Robert told me you asked about me. That is why you don't see me at church. It is so difficult to get in and out of a buggy and then to get into the school or the church that I don't really want to go. My brothers have offered to carry me, but I don't want that. I don't want other people to have to wait on me, and I definitely don't want other children to think I am a weakling."

Her voice began to choke, and I saw tears well up her in eyes. I didn't know what to say. There was a long pause as I watched a tear slowly escape her eye and drift down her cheek. She sniffled and wiped away the tear.

"I'm sorry, I didn't mean to bore you with that old story. I just saw you looking at my legs, and I thought you ought to know."

A slight grin appeared on her face, and she changed the subject.

"Tell me about Darlin'. Is she your favorite?"

I was speechless. I never knew anyone who could not walk; at least, not anyone my age. I had a thousand questions. *Did it hurt then? Did it still hurt now? How old where you? Your legs don't move at all? Do you always have to stay in that chair? Couldn't you still get on a horse?* I was afraid to ask. Was it because I did not want to embarrass her or was I afraid of learning the answer? I became very sad for her.

"Billy," she said, as she tried to find my eyes. She had wheeled in front of me and to the right, trying to intercept my vision. I was gazing somewhere far away and beyond this place. Suddenly I saw her before me, and it jolted me back to reality.

"Yes?" I sputtered.

"Darlin', your horse, is she your favorite?"

"Darlin'? Oh, Darlin', not really my favorite. I had her since I was little. She was really my dad's horse." I didn't want to talk about Darlin', I wanted to talk about Samantha.

"How about Princess? I see you on her sometimes, too. Is she your favorite?"

"No, I love my horses, and I love to take care of them, but my favorite doesn't even belong to me - at least not yet. One day he will." I again began to gaze off into the distance.

"Who is he, Billy? Does he belong to someone?"

I thought to myself, *Who does he belong to?* I think maybe he belonged to the mighty wind; or maybe he belonged to the great mountains; or to the rushing rivers. He definitely did not belong to any man - or boy. At least not yet.

"I don't know who he belongs to," I said. "I've seen him in the hills. I think he's just a wild one."

"Then you will get him one day, Billy, you will." I looked at Samantha, and a feeling of determination came over me. *Yes, I will get him and he will be mine.*

Samantha and I talked a lot about horses. She loved them as much as I did. She must have really loved Olivia. I knew it must have made Samantha very sad to lose her. But to lose her horse *and* to lose her legs - I couldn't imagine that. I tried to see myself in that chair. She could not go upstairs or out to the yard because of the steps. She was stuck on just the porch and the first floor of her house. And she couldn't go to school. I guess if I couldn't go the school, I would really miss it. I wondered if Samantha wanted me to ask more questions about her legs. She did not mention it again, and I didn't either. I was enjoying my time with her. She seemed like a normal person. I had believed some not-so-pleasant thoughts about her. She really is like everybody else, except more special.

We continued to talk about horses. But after a while, I guessed I started to feel more comfortable with Samantha. I began to tell her some of the tales I had heard about my dad. I told her about my dad taking cattle to market many times without any trailhands, and how he could handle many more cattle than he had now to take on the trail. The only reason he needed trailhands was for the company. Sometimes he would hire on a fella who was down and out on his luck, just to give him a job and a paycheck, and get him on his feet again. I told her the story I heard about my dad building a barn for a neighbor all by himself in only three days. Then I mentioned the story I heard about the drought in Mexico when my dad dug a well over one hundred feet deep to get to water for a village. Some of the stories I had heard were too farfetched to repeat, but she wanted to hear them anyway. So I told her about the one someone had told a group of men in front of the General Store; about how a tornado came across the plains toward a town in Arkansas and my dad used a lasso to rope it and hold it long enough for the wind to die out. We both laughed at that one, but I felt I could trust her not to laugh at me, or make fun of what I said.

Before I knew it, the time had slipped by. I had not thought of anything else except talking with Samantha. Then I remembered my mom had told me to get the letter from Mr. Jacobs. *What time was it?* I got here around three o'clock, so it must have been close to four o'clock and I needed to get to town before Mr. Jacob left his store.

Samantha could see I was a little concerned about something, and she asked,

"Billy, what is it?"

"My mom got a letter yesterday and I needed to get to town to pick it up. I think it must be from my dad."

"Do you think it's still there?" She looked through the window to a large standup clock near the stairs. "I can see the time from here, and it's after six."

"After six?" I screeched. My heart sunk. No, Mr. Jacobs would not be there. It was too late. I missed getting the letter. *What would I say to Mom?* I knew I could get it on Monday, but she was looking forward to that letter today, especially since it had been at the store since Saturday. My whole body began to melt into the swing, and I felt a sickness in the bottom of my stomach. I hated to disappoint my mom. She was so cheery when she found out about the letter. I knew this was going to make her sad.

"I have to go," I abruptly stated. I jumped from the swing and headed down the porch steps.

"Are you leaving now?" said Samantha I could tell from her voice she was almost pleading for me to stay.

"Yes, I have to get that letter," I said, and I was around the house and on Darlin' in one quick swoop. "I will see you soon, I promise."

I could see Samantha waving to me as I passed onto the road. I felt like I had promised my mom, too. I had promised to get that letter - and get that letter I would.

CHAPTER 9

TROUBLE AT THE BANK

I am not sure I had ever ridden Darlin' that hard before. I believed she could feel my body tense as I pushed her harder and harder to go faster and faster. It seemed I could not go fast enough. The shadows were getting longer and, even if I had gotten the letter, it would definitely be nightfall when I got home. *Oh, please, Mr. Jacobs, be there,* I said to myself.

As I rode into town, I knew right away he was not there. No one was anywhere. The whole town looked deserted. Sunday night was the night to stay home. Nothing was open on Sunday. Most folks had gone to church that morning. Sometimes it lasted into the afternoon and by the time everyone had gone home, had their meal and cleared the table, Sunday night became a time to rest up for the week ahead. I was never out this late on a Sunday night, and especially never in town. Even the occasional travelers who would pass through town were nowhere to be seen.

As I slowly walked Darlin' to the General Store, I got a strange shiver up my back, like something was not right. I felt I needed to hide, and I became a little scared. I tied Darlin' up to the post behind Mr. Jacobs' store, and walked to the front. Suddenly, I noticed I was not alone after all. As the sun began moving below the distant hills in the west, I could see shadows moving across the street like black, silent images darting among the buildings. *Had they seen me? Had they heard me ride up on Darlin'? Did they know I was here?* I froze against the corner of the General Store. *Why were they so quiet?* Then I realized - they must have been up to no good. Something bad was going to happen.

As I moved across the front of the General Store, I realized they were men headed to the bank. *A bank robbery in this town?* That had never happened before. *Where was the sheriff? Where was the deputy?* I was afraid to yell for help - there was no one in the town to hear me. Once I commenced to think about it, I realized that if *anyone* was going to rob *anyplace* in our town, Sunday night seemed likely the best time to do it. Now, I figured, someone else had found that out, too. As I stared out at the town in the dim light of the setting sun, my eyes soon became adjusted and I could start to make out the shape of three men in front of Mr. Trunipseed's bank. *That's right! That was Mr. Turnipseed's bank!* I slowly sunk down to the ground at the corner of Mr. Jacobs' storefront. I then realized I could get closer to the bank if I snuck around back and crossed the street near the livery stables.

As I passed through the stalls, I saw several long strands of rope on the wall. I felt I should stop these robbers - but how? I didn't think I had time for a plan right then. I would just take the rope and make it up as I went. At that moment, I saw a match being struck and a small lantern was lit, giving a soft glow through the door of the bank. As I slowly crept across the street, I could see one person standing near the door. He was not looking my way; he was looking down toward the sheriff's office. I saw my chance to get closer, and soon I was standing in the alley between the bank and the barbershop. I hugged the side of the bank as I stepped quietly to the front. As I got near the sidewalk, I realized I was so close, I could hear the man breathe. He had a deep raspy breath, and a low hacking cough. He moved toward my corner. I quickly squatted as low as I could, hiding near the edge of the raised sidewalk.

He was now right above me, and I prayed he would not see me. As I inched ever so close, I could even smell his breath. It was a mixture of strong tobacco and heavy liquor. I could hear him chewing, and then I saw him spit. It landed so close to me I thought he would see me. I held my breath for fear he could hear my heart beating in my chest. I closed my eyes and waited for him to find me. As he paced back and forth in front of the bank, I could hear the shuffle of his boots and the soft clang of his spurs. And, just at the moment I knew he would step on me, a horrible sound of groans came from inside the bank. The man quickly turned around and headed to the front door.

"Keep it down in there," he tried to whisper, but his harsh voice was much too loud. "Ya never know who might be out and about."

I heard another voice from inside respond. This voice was more muffled and he sounded like his mouth was full of chewing tobacco.

"He ain't tellin' me nothin'."

And then, as if talking to someone else, the voice inside declared, "You either tell us how to get into this safe, or you're a goner!"

"Get'im to talk, Zeke, we ain't got all night." The man with the raspy-voice said.

I heard the muffled voice yell back, "I told you not to use names, you fool! Now we'll have to kill'm for sure!"

"I *will* kill him even if he don't tell. Let's see if the butt of this rifle gets'm goin'."

Then I heard this awful sound of a thud crashing against flesh and bone. I heard a body crash to the floor. I heard more moaning, and I began to feel sick at the sounds of pain.

Who were they talking to? Who were they beating and threatening to kill? The raspy-voiced man was now inside the bank. He had forgotten to keep a watch on the front, and I had an opportunity to crawl around the front and look inside. I slowly edged my body forward to the opened door. I raised my head so that I could use one eye to look inside. I saw two men standing over a body as it writhed on the floor, and they were arguing back and forth.

I couldn't hear exactly what they were saying. I was intently watching the man who had rolled over on his stomach and was beginning to very slowly crawl toward the door. I could hear his moans of pain from the butt of the gun that had slashed against his body. I glanced up.

The two men were still arguing and they did not notice what was happening. I wanted to help the one on the floor, but I didn't know what to do. I looked around and I saw their horses. An idea to rescue the one on the floor jumped in my head. Still squatting, I took two long steps, and I was off the sidewalk, next to the horses. I quickly assured them by rubbing them gently along their necks and chests. I tied a rope around one of the hitching posts and just as quickly, I brought the other end of the rope back to the front door of the bank. As I glanced at the man on the floor, I could now see his face. I was shocked! I knew him!

It was Clark, Mr. Turnipseed's other son! He worked in the bank, too! They were trying to get him to open the safe and then they would probably kill him! I *had* to get him out of there. I could see blood covering his clothes and he seemed dazed. With the light of the moon now showing the way, Clark crawled to the threshold of the door. When he looked up, he seemed shocked to see me outside the bank. His jaw dropped and he was about to speak when I raised my finger to my lips. I showed him the rope and slipped the end toward him. As he slowly eased out of the bank, he took the rope and began to wrap it around his hands several times. He seemed to understand my plan.

As soon as he was ready, he nodded to me. I was almost ready to pull him away from the bank when I heard the men talking.

"Well, we're just gonna have to blast it open," decided the raspy-voiced one.

"Go get the dynamite," said Zeke, the muffled voice one, "I'll clear out a place to put it."

Now the raspy voiced one was heading out the door, right toward me! We had to stop him. With a nod, both Clark and I held the rope very tightly and, just as the man began to exit the door, we both pulled the rope taut and caught his foot. We pulled up and back as hard as we could, and we sent his body flying out the door, face first, soaring over the sidewalk and into the street below. His gun flew from his hand, far into the distant night.

From inside the bank, we heard the muffled-voice one say,

"What the –" and he too began to run out of the bank. Again, Clark and I used the rope to trip up the robber. He too, went flying, landing in the street right next to his partner in crime. His gun was not flung very far but landed in the street not far from me. By now, Clark had recovered enough to climb to his knees and moved next to me. He picked up the gun and I helped him to his feet. We both walked to the street to see the two robbers knocked out cold. Clark now spoke for the first time.

"Bring that rope and let's tie them up." I could hear the pain in his voice.

Very quickly we used the rope I had brought, and we tied the feet and hands both men as tight as we could and then we tied them to each other. Once the two bandits were bound together, we both sat back down against the front of the bank. Now we could breathe. At the same time, Clark and I gave out a great sigh of relief and then nervously laughed at what we had done together. Clark began to wipe the blood from his face. He looked at me, smiled, and said,

"You are a hero, young fellow." He reached out to shake my hand. "You saved the bank and the money in this town, and you saved my life." He shook my hand and did not let go for a long time. "By the way, who are you?"

"I'm Billy."

He reached to shake my hand again. "Nice to meet you, Billy. I'm . . ."

"Clark Turnipseed," I said before he could.

"You know me?" he questioned.

"Yes, sir," I responded politely.

"How?" he quizzed.

"I met you at your house for dinner one Sunday."

"Oh, yes, I know you! Billy, it is! You are the one that Samantha has been talking about so much! Did you finally get to the house today? I heard you were coming. Sorry I was not there. As you can see, I was a little detained." He looked around the bank and at the two robbers, and he continued without me saying a word.

"These two ambushed me on the way to the livery stable when I was just outside of town." He closed his eyes, and I watched him slump against the wall. "My horse had lost a shoe and I needed it fixed. I was not far from town so I was heading here when they jumped me. They held me for quite a few hours until dark. Then they tried to force me to open the safe."

As I sat there listening to him, I now realized how scared I was. I looked at my hands, and they were shaking. My whole body was trembling, and I could not control it. Blood was still all over Clark's face. I thought he was starting to feel the strain of what had happened, too. He opened his eyes and turned slowly towards me. I saw him trying to talk, but I spoke before him.

"You need someone to look at that nasty wound." I tried to stand up, but I slipped back down from the weakness in my knees. Clark caught me as I fell across him and rolled to the other side. We both began to chuckle. We were both too weak to get up.

"Hey, I'll be fine. I was just thinking how lucky I was that you happened along when you did. You saved my life!"

Clark paused for a moment and then asked, "How old are you?"

"Thirteen," I answered.

"Thirteen," he repeated. "Well, I'm twenty and I could not have done what you did."

He thanked me again, a tone of great gratitude in his voice. "Thank you. Had it not been for you, I would be dead on that floor," he said as he motioned into the bank, "and this place would have been blown to pieces. Maybe the whole town would have been burned down."

With that, he slowly rose to his knees and then to his feet. He reached down and helped me stand up, too. We noticed the two robbers were beginning to come to. With the gun he had picked up, Clark fired it into the air to wake up any of the folk who might be living near town. He told me to find the sheriff or the deputy while he watched the robbers until help arrived. I grabbed Darlin' and I started down the street and out of town. I saw several men coming from the north end of town. They must have heard the gunshots.

"What's goin' on?" one yelled out as he pulled his suspenders up over his shoulders.

"Someone tried to rob the bank," I replied. "Where is the sheriff?"

"He's out of town," he answered back, "but the deputy should be here soon. Couple of horses were stolen this morning from the Anderson's spread, and he went to check on it." I knew the Anderson horses. I thought back and I realized the two horses the thieves had were from the Anderson spread. I quickly rode out toward the Anderson's and, before I got very far, I ran into Deputy Mills. He could tell I was riding hard, and he rode quickly to meet me.

"Who goes there?" he yelled out.

"It's me. It's Billy Pecos."

"What's happening, Billy?" he called as we met.

"Someone tried to rob the bank. I think it was the same ones who stole the Anderson horses." Before I could get it all out, Deputy Mills was already headed full stride back to town.

Darlin' was tired. I tried to keep up with him, but we loped into town long after he had already made it. From the outskirts of town, I could see several more of the townspeople had gathered in the street. They did not see me, but as I rode closer in the darkness, I could hear my name being bandied around.

"Yea, it was Billy, Bill Pecos' son," one shouted.

"Clark would have been a dead man, had it not been for Billy," yelled another.

"We would have lost everything in the bank, had it not been for Pecos' son," still another shouted out.

And still others were joining the chorus:

"Deputy, that young man is a real hero!"

"Sure is a fine young man, that Billy!"

"Mighty brave, I'd say!"

I sat on Darlin', motionless. I did not know what to think. No one had noticed I was on my horse, just within earshot. *I'm a hero? Brave? Fine young man?* I did not know what to do. Darlin' was hot and tired from the long run. I rubbed her flank, and I could feel the foamy sweat on her. I needed to cool her off and Clark was now in good hands. I turned and headed for home. Many emotions were bouncing inside me. I felt strange about what happened at the bank and with Clark and what the people were saying, and I also felt strange because the reason I went to town in the first place was to get my mom's letter. And I was going home without it.

CHAPTER 10

TROUBLE AT HOME

It was now very late, and I could tell my mom was still up. The same lamp she kept on when she was expecting Dad to come home was on the kitchen table. I could see its soft glow through the curtains. I knew she would be worried, and it was my fault. Not only worried, but she would be angry at me about the letter. I didn't know what to tell her. I felt bad because I knew I would disappoint her. What could I say? 'Mom, I forgot,' or 'Mom, a girl is more important than you,' or 'Mom, Darlin' got sick and . . .' No, I couldn't lie. She always knew when I was lying. Some people thought I was a good liar, like whenever I used to tell some of those stories about my dad. For me, lying was never a good idea.

I reached the gate and dismounted Darlin'. We had ridden home slow so I could let her cool off. I led her in the stall, gave her some new hay and a bucket of feed and water. She would be fine. I would finish taking care of her tomorrow. I closed the gate and dragged myself up the back steps. I couldn't believe how tired I was, and I still had a lot of explaining to do. *Please be understanding, Mom,* I said to myself. *Please don't be mad,* I practiced. I reached for the door, and it was unlocked. I turned the latch and pushed it open. I saw my mom at the table with a handkerchief in her hand. Her face was redder and more covered in tears than I had ever seen it. Her eyes were glassy and very puffy. Seeing my mom like this pricked my heart, and I began to feel very bad.

"Mom," I said, commencing to speak. She jumped up and rushed to me, wrapping her arms around me, pulling my face into the curve of her neck. She was holding me so tightly, I could hardly say a word.

"Billy? Where have you been? I thought something had happened to you! I was so worried!"

I tried to speak again, but my mouth was pressed into her shoulder and my words were only muffled sounds. She finally released me enough for me to talk.

"Mom, I'm sorry, I didn't get your letter from Mr. Jacobs. Please don't be angry. I tried, I really tried." She released her hug, but placed her large hands on my shoulders and held me facing her.

"The letter? I have the letter, Billy! When you didn't show up at Mr. Jacobs', he decided to drop it off himself."

You have the letter? I just went through being involved in a bank robbery because I went to get your letter, and you already had it? I didn't know what to say. Mom let me go and returned to the table. She fell into the chair in a way that let me know she was very tired and very upset.

"You're not upset with me?" I questioned.

"I was very worried, like any mom would be, but, Billy, you are growing up, and I knew you could take care of yourself. You are Bill Pecos' son."

Now I was confused. If she wasn't worried about me, why was she crying? Was there something in the letter? I had to ask.

"Mom, the letter. Was it from Dad?"

"It was. He's in Canada. The letter was sent from there. It just took a long time getting here. He sent it in early March and here it is near June and we are just now getting it."

Her handkerchief was soaked from wiping her tears. She tried to pretend she was all right, but I knew better. Dad was not coming home. I figured that out. I wanted to know what was in the letter. It was lying opened on the table, and I moved to sit beside her and, hopefully, find out what it said. As I did, she picked up the letter and handed it to me.

"You read it, Billy. There is something in it that is important to you." She pointed to a part that had my name, and I began to read out loud.

"I hope all is well with Billy. Tell him I am on the biggest cattle drive of my life. We found a great market for our beef - Europe and Asia. Tell Billy, we are going to try to feed the millions and millions of people in China and Japan and England and France and those other countries who hanker for American beef. I wish he were here. The country is beautiful. We are starting the grandest ranch you could ever imagine. Why, Texas could not hold all the beef we gonna have if they was standing side by side and double tall. I hope you get this letter soon so Billy can get our cattle to market. It's important. You will need the money to get all the supplies you will need to set you through the winter. Tell him good luck and my prayers are with him. I know he can do it. Remind him that he is Bill Pecos' son.

I love you all. Give Daniel and Carrie a great big Pecos hug for me. With all the cattle we are moving, I may not be home before winter. Why, the snow is gonna be so deep here . . . ."

I didn't finish reading the letter. I tried to think and understand what was happening, but I was too tired. There were so many thoughts going through my head. At the same time, I felt as if my whole body was spinning in a twister. I placed the letter back on the table in front of my mom. I wasn't sure she even saw me, but, as I began to get up to walk away, she touched my hand and started to talk.

"Billy . . ." she stopped as if trying to think of what to say but no words came. I knew what she was thinking and I finished her thought.

"I know, Mom. I gotta take the cattle to market, and I gotta go tomorrow."

"But, Billy, your . . ."

"School. I know. It'll have to wait." I was too tired to continue. We both knew it was already late in the year to take cattle to market and the prices would be low and I may be gone for four months or more. If I left now I could definitely make it back before the snow came to the northern hills. I remembered my dad telling me that it took him almost three weeks just to get to the Oklahoma Territory. That would mean I would be traveling ten to twelve miles a day with my herd. It would be at least another six weeks from there to Dodge City, Kansas. That would mean as least nine weeks there and, it I hurried, eight weeks back; *if* the weather was good and *if* there were no Indian or rustler or stampede problems. And *if* there was enough water and the rivers weren't swollen nor were they dry. With good luck, I could return in four months; with bad luck, it could be five months or more before I could get back home. All these thoughts were beginning to make my head swim again. As I tried to walk away again, she called to me once more,

"Billy, you're the man of this house when you father is not here. I know you will do what is right. You are a brave young man, and I love you." Tears came to her eyes again and she turned away. I shuffled off to the loft, too tired to even change my clothes. I fell into the bed, collapsing across it.

A *brave young man*. That was the second time I heard that tonight. I didn't feel brave; at least, not like my father.

CHAPTER 11

EVERYBODY KNEW THE STORY

Why was there so much noise on a Monday morning? I slowly rolled over and realized there was a lot of light coming into the house. What time was it? It had to be late. I was never in bed this time of the day. It was light outside, and I could see the sun shining into the house. I had chores. I had my horses to take care of. I tried to get up, but my body was sore, and it ached. *Why did I feel so weak and dizzy? What happened to me last night?* Slowly the events of the day crept back into my mind. Samantha . . . the bank.... Clark . . . the letter . . . my dad not coming home . . . taking the cattle to market by myself . . . *Was that all in just one day?*

It seemed like I had lived a year in just the last day. Was all that just a dream, or did I really experience what I remembered? I still heard noise downstairs. Was it just my family making all that commotion or were there others downstairs? I looked around and saw that my brother's and sister's beds were empty and made up. It must have been late if they were already up and gone.

I pulled my feet across the bed and placed them on the floor. Warmth seeped into my soles from the fireplace below because of the cooking my mother had been doing. Now I could tell it was really late. I needed to balance myself to stand and, as I raised my head, I took a deep breath. *I have to get downstairs. I have to get going.* I was trying to convince myself. My head was beginning to clear. As I dragged my feet to the ladder, I could hear the voices better. I thought I recognized them. One was... the Sheriff, and the other was... Mr. Turnipseed? *What were they doing here? Was I in trouble? Did something happen to Samantha?* I turned and took a backward step down the ladder. I had to be careful to take one step at a time, since I was still a little weak-kneed and light headed.

"Here he comes! Billy, I didn't want to wake you, but these gentlemen wanted sorely to see you!" my mom said to me. She seemed in a better spirit today. There was a bit of joy in her voice. I was glad.

I was not down the ladder yet, and both men began to talk to me at the same time. I did not know which one was speaking.

"Good morning, Billy"

"Good morning, young man."

"We are glad to see you are safe."

"No one saw you after you went for the Deputy."

"We were so worried about you."

"You saved the day."

"And Clark, too!"

"That's right! You're a hero young fellow!"

When I reached the bottom of the ladder, I turned around and Mom was there right in front of me. She gave me a hug so big I felt like my bones would crack. She still had tears, but they seemed to be happy tears.

"Billy, Billy, Billy," my mom said with the widest smile she ever had on her face, "You never told me last night what happened! I am so proud of you!"

Mr. Turnipseed pushed past the Sheriff and stood next to my mom. He reached down and grabbed my hand and began to shake it so hard I thought he was going to pull it off.

"My family and I owe you a lot, young man, or William, or can I call you Billy?" gushed Mr. Turnipseed. When he finally let go of my hand, he said, "My son tells me that if it weren't for you he would be dead today and the bank would have been robbed."

"I don't know who will be the more famous of you two now," bellowed the Sheriff as he, too, stepped up close to me, "you or your father. Why, I'm not sure 'ol Pecos ever saved a life and a bank at the same time!"

I was overwhelmed. I thought my head was clearing, but now it began to swim again.

"May I sit down?" I pleaded.

"Of course!" "Yes!" "Why yes, indeed." I heard them all, eager to answer. The Sheriff immediately grabbed a chair and pushed it under me, as Mr. Turnipseed and Mom held each an arm and helped me to be seated. I took a deep breath and tried to speak. In anticipation, they stopped jabbering and they all leaned forward as if they were waiting for some remarkable announcement. I was now wide-awake, and all the events of yesterday were flooding my mind. The time I spent with Samantha. The quick ride to town to get the letter. The bank robbers. Clark.

I looked up to Mr. Turnipseed and asked, "Is Clark fine?"

"Oh, yes, except for a nasty bump on his head, he is fit as a fiddle, thanks to you!" he glowed. He looked at the other two and stated matter-of-factly, as if he had not told them before, "He saved my son's life!"

"Mom," I said as I looked up at her, and, again, all three leaned toward me, hanging on every word. I wanted to say something about Dad. I wanted to talk to her about having to leave and take the cattle to market. I wanted to talk to her about Carrie and Robert. I had not gone anywhere yet, and I was feeling very lonely for my family. I could feel a sadness and a loneliness begin in the pit of my stomach and slowly take over my body. I wanted to hug my mom and do the same with my little brother and sister. But I couldn't. Not with the other men standing around. At that very moment, all I wanted was family.

"Are you hungry?" Mom asked, as she tried to anticipate what I wanted. She had prepared me breakfast already, and she quickly slid a plate of biscuits with cream butter and a large slice of beef jerky. It smelled good, but I was not hungry. I did not want to disappoint her, so I nodded in agreement. I reached for a biscuit and took a bite. I could see the approval on her face. Maybe she noticed that I was thinking something else. She grabbed a chair, and Mr. Turnipseed helped her pull it toward me. Our chairs were together, and she sat as close to me as she could.

"Everything will be wonderful, Billy," she began, "I know when you came home last night, I was very sad and a little upset. I didn't know what was going to happen with our family with your dad so far away, and, and, well," she paused, "I will let Mr. Turnipseed and the Sheriff tell you."

As she moved away from me, the two men traded glances to see who would start first. Finally, the Sheriff spoke,

"Billy, you know those two men were wanted criminals you captured last night?"

Wanted criminals? I captured? What about them? I thought.

"There might even be a reward for them," he continued. He glanced at my mom and smiled broadly. He looked back at me and said, "And if there is, we are giving it to you and Clark! I'll send a letter to Abilene to find out. We should know by the end of next month!"

All three moved back and stood up straight and basked in the statement that was just uttered. They all seemed to be waiting for my response. I had too many things going through my mind to even ask a question.

"Billy, that's not all," whispered Mom, and Mr. Turnipseed jumped in the conversation.

"No sir, young William, I mean, Billy. Because you helped save the bank and for your heroic effort last night, there is a reward for that too," he boasted, "For a young fellow your age, it'll be a tidy sum! Just as soon as we get the bank cleaned up, the doors repaired and back opened in a few days, just come on down for your reward!"

"Why, that's all the town is talking about now - 'Billy the hero', and you are a hero!" the Sheriff said with his chest puffed out and his eyes looking off into the distance. He turned to my mom and added, "You must be very proud of him!"

With that, all three began to chat incoherently with each other. At least, I could not tell what exactly they were saying. It was all about the bank and the robbery and Clark, and maybe a reward, and it was all so jumbled that I didn't even want to understand. I took one of the biscuits in front of me and tried another bite. I had forgotten I had not eaten since after church yesterday. The taste was good but I was not hungry. I nibbled some more of the biscuit and then chewed off a piece of jerky. I tried to swallow, but it was hard to get down. *Why was there so much excitement?* I did not do any more than anyone else would do. The reward sounded great, and maybe it could help our family some. But I still had responsibilities and my dad expected me to do my part. I still had the cattle to take to market.

Just at that moment, I no longer felt tired, but I began to feel a little embarrassed with all the attention. *What did he say? That's all the town is talking about? What were people going to say to me?* Already, some of them thought I was a liar for telling some of stories about my dad. *Will they believe this story . . . about me? How will I live with this?* All I could think about doing right now was going out to my stables and being with my horses. I looked down and saw I still had my same clothes on from yesterday. It didn't matter. I started to get up and leave the table, and all conversation stopped.

Mom asked me, "Where are you going, dear?"

"To the stables, Mom, to take care of the horses."

"But, son . . ," called out the Sheriff as he moved towards me. But my mom turned and placed an arm in front of him, and she stopped him in his tracks.

"That's fine, Billy. Why don't you take care of them now?" she said softly to me.

I moved out the door. One thing about my mom was that she understood me, and she always let me take care of those things that were important to me.

I went to see Darlin' first. I had ridden her hard last night and she needed to be rubbed down and washed. I filled a bucket from the well and found one of the old shirts of my dad's that I always used to wash the horses. Even though I'd washed them hundreds of times with that old shirt, I believed the horses could still smell my dad when I used it. It seemed to make them calm. They knew him and felt safe around him. I knew the feeling. I was thinking earlier how much I wanted to be around my family right now. I missed and wanted my dad too. I remembered the letter from last night, and I became very sad. *Why did he have to be gone? Were we not important to him? Didn't he care about us?* The more I thought, the angrier I became. *Why was I getting angry?* I wanted to kick something, throw something. I wanted to go outside and yell at the top of my lungs. *This is not fair!*

But then, I took a breath, a deep breath, and then another and I closed my eyes long enough to say, "Okay God. I can't do this alone. Please help me." I just missed my dad. I was not mad at him. I just missed him. And now I had to take the cattle to market myself. I was dreaming of the day I could ride with him all the way to Kansas on a cattle drive, but I never knew I would have to do it all by myself. And for that, I was really going to miss my dad.

12

PREPARING FOR
THE CATTLE DRIVE

The strong smell of meat cooking woke me up early. Yesterday had gone by quickly. I had so much to do to get ready – hay to bale, stalls to clean, water to haul, cattle to move, animals to feed and repairs to make that I had not planned to do this soon. I didn't have time to think much about the reward, or what had happened the day before. I had to get ready for today. It was still dark out, and my mom must have gotten up in the middle of the night to start cooking. I didn't feel as tired as I did yesterday. I rose and I could see Daniel and Carrie still asleep in their beds. The lamp my mom had burning below cast an eerie shadow across the ceiling of our house. Glancing down the stairs I could tell the embers in the fireplace had now burned low and did not give off much light.

I thought back about the events of the day before - about the visit from the Sheriff and Mr. Turnipseed. I felt badly now that I walked out on them, but I had to get some of my chores done to be gone from home for such a long trip. I enjoyed being out in the barn. I was not used to all the attention I was getting. I felt I needed to get away from that. And staying busy in the barn helped me not to think about being away so long from my family. During the whole time I was there yesterday, I did not think much about what had happened the last few days. My only thoughts were about preparing to leave and the drive.

I remembered the tales my dad would tell me about the trip. He would always tell us the story every time he returned. It was often the same, but it did not matter, I liked hearing them over and over. Now I was glad because maybe those tales would help me get through this. I remembered him telling about the flat lands, the valleys, and ridges he would pass. I remembered him telling me about the rivers and creeks that he would have to wade or even swim through. The more I thought about it, the more I remembered.

"Follow the river east to the settlement and then north," he would say, "You can't miss it."

Yesterday I was feeling a little scared, but, as I recalled the stories from my dad, I could sense a feeling of confidence swelling up inside of me. *I can do this,* I thought to myself. *I can do this.*

I definitely had more energy today than yesterday. I bounded down the ladder. I had no idea what time it was.

"Good morning," I heard my mom whisper so as not to wake the little ones, "You seem to be in much better mood this morning." She paused as she set a place for me at the table. "You hardly said a word to anyone after you left for the barn yesterday. Did you get the horses ready?"

"Yes, ma'am," I answered.

"And the cattle," she added, "are they in the corral and ready?"

"Yes, ma'am," I said again.

That was all I was able to do since I had awakened so late yesterday. I remembered Mom bringing supper out to me late in the day, and, by the time I got back in the house, Daniel and Carrie were already in bed, but I could hear them taking so they were still awake. Everyone pretty much left me alone yesterday. I guessed it was good. I had a lot to think about, but now I was sorry I did not spend more time with my mom and brother and sister. I would be gone for many months, and I was going to surely miss them.

I saw bags sitting on the table. They were the bags my dad used to carry the food my mom had cooked for him on his trips. Now I was going to use them. I knew what she had fixed. She had been cooking thin strips of beef jerky for several weeks, anticipating my dad would be here. She had made dozens of hard sourdough biscuits and packed bags of coffee, sugar and salt and flour and pork fat. She had tied together the coffeepot and cups with an iron skillet and spoons sitting on the table ready to be wrapped. It seemed like a lot of grub for just one person. She must have been thinking my dad and his hired hands would be using them. I did not have a hired hand. It would just be me.

There was no one I could ask. Everyone my age would be heading to school before I would return. All the older cowhands were already hired out and on the trail. They would not be back for many weeks and I could not wait that long. And I definitely was not going to ask Thomas or Silas! I could never put up with them on the trail. I could just see them high-tailing it home after just a few days – homesick for their mommies!

Could I even do this? I thought to myself. *My dad seemed to believe in me. Could I believe in myself? Did my dad need help? I doubt it. He could have done the trail ride all by himself.*

I heard my mom talking to herself as she checked over all my supplies and continued to pack everything. She had set out a biscuit for me, as well as a strip of jerky and a cup of hot coffee. I didn't usually drink coffee, but this was a special morning. It was just like when my dad was ready to hit the trail, my mom would give him the same breakfast – biscuit, jerky and coffee. Also, there on the table was the blanket my dad was given by a famous Indian chief. My mom saw me looking at the blanket.

"It's yours. Even before you were born, it was a gift to be given to you."

"But this is Dad's special blanket." I said.

"It's special because it was given for you from one of your father's best friends."

I smiled as I rolled my bedding up in it.

It was the morning I was to round up my cattle and head for the trail. I finished the biscuit and coffee, and I took the rest of the jerky with me as I headed out to the barn. It was still dark, but the sky was clear, and the moon was almost full, so it lit up the walk out to the barn. I did not need to light a lantern to see my way. I knew where everything was. I had left Darlin' an extra helping of feed last night, and she had eaten it all. I put on her bridle, and in the quiet of the night, she stood there and let me saddle her. Once I had Darlin' ready, I put a bridle on Princess, and I brought them both to the back porch. I would ride Darlin' and I would let Princess carry my goods.

As I stopped on the porch, I realized I would not be back here for a long time. Once I got on my horse, I would be riding out to the corral to get the cattle and head directly to the trail. Often, I would be in this spot with my dad. He would be gone for months. I would ride out with him and his hired hands and all of us would round up the cattle and head out to the trail. But all those times before, I would be back by nightfall of that evening. Now I was in this spot again. I had always looked forward to one day riding out with my dad and not coming back until the drive was done and we came back together. But that was not going to happen; at least not this year. I was going to have to do it by myself.

While I had been getting the horses ready, Mom had brought the supplies out to the porch, and I began to load them onto Princess. I tossed these large pouches over her back, and tied them around her girth and around her neck. As I filled them, the sound of clanking cups and pots broke the silence of the early morning hours. I tried to be quiet, but to no avail. I heard the backdoor open, and out popped Daniel and Carrie. Both were standing on the porch in their bare feet. They were rubbing their eyes and yawning without making a sound. Mom came out and stood behind them. I looked up and apologized, "I'm sorry I made so much noise. I didn't mean to wake you up so early. Why don't you two go back to bed?"

"Billy, you did not wake them. I did," said Mom. "They begged me last night to wake them before you left so they can tell you goodbye."

I told each one how much I would miss them and how when I came back they would have grown so much. I told them to take care of their mother and obey. I told them to be good in school, if I don't get back in time. I told them to remember their chores.

My mom looked at me and said, "Billy, I have something for you to take with you." She reached into the pocket of her apron and pulled out a watch on a chain. "This belonged to my father's father - your great-grandfather. Right before he died, when you were just a baby, he told me to give this to you. I was going to wait until you finished school and you went out on your own." Her voice started to break, but she continued, "Well, I think you are old enough already and you are definitely heading out on your own, and . . ." she stopped, and, as she covered her mouth with one hand, she handed the watch to me with the other. As I took it from her, she raced back into the house. "Don't forget this."

I could hear her rummaging through the bin near the fireplace. She emerged from the house with our family rifle, and handed it to me along with a box of shells.

"Mom," I pleaded, "I can't take it. You may need it here"

"No, you will need it more. We will be fine without it." She started to chuckle and added, "We haven't used it all year, and you will need it to hunt with."

By now I had packed all the supplies, and I was ready to ride. As I stood there looking at my family, I was full of emotions. It was hard to tell them goodbye, but I knew if I were to leave and not say goodbye, I would be miserable until I got back. As I took a step towards the porch, Carrie ran and leaped off the top of the porch, jumping into my arms. Daniel ran down the steps and threw his arms around my waist. Both of them hugged me as hard as they could. Carrie began to sob and Mom walked down the steps and pulled my sister to herself.

Daniel looked up at me and asked, "Can I go with you? I can help. You don't have anyone to go with you."

He had the saddest face I had ever seen on him. I took his face into my palms and I got on one knee in front of him.

"Daniel," I said, "do you remember when Dad would leave on these trips?"

"Yes," he answered.

"And," I asked, "do you remember what he would say to me every time before he left?"

"Yes, he said, 'you are the man of the house now'."

"Well," I continued, "Dad is not here, and I am leaving this time, and I will say the same to you. You are the man of the house now."

Daniel's face beamed and he nodded his head in agreement as he realized he was needed here. His whole countenance started to glow as he began to see himself growing up. As I rose to my feet, I looked into the eyes of my Mom that were now filled with tears.

"Billy," she said, "We want to pray with you."

The four of us squeezed together, arms around each other, heads bowed and our eyes closed.

"Father in Heaven, be with Billy on this journey. Send Your angels to protect him and guide him and please, Lord, bring him back safely." She paused for a moment, and continued, "And, Lord, be with my husband and their father and keep him safe too. Amen." We continued to hug for a moment longer, but then I knew it was time to let go and start my 'journey' as Mom said.

"Goodbye, Mom. Goodbye, Daniel. Goodbye, Carrie," I said as I fought back the tears from my own eyes.

"God's speed, my Billy," my mom's voice cracked.

My family was huddled together in the light of the early dawn, the sunlight trying to peek over the eastern mountains. They stood there watching me leave. I waved and they waved back. God's speed, my mom said to me. *Yes*, I said to myself, *God's speed.*

CHAPTER 13

STARTING ON THE TRAIL

By the time I had gathered the entire herd, the sun was beginning to peek over the hills in front of me, and soon it broke through and was shining right into my face. As we moved onto the trail, I began to count the cattle I had with me. I remembered my dad telling me how he would always lose a few longhorns on the drive. Some would die from wounds or sickness, and some would just wander off from the herd. It would make me sad to hear that. I did not want to lose any that were with me. I counted one hundred forty-seven - almost too many for just one man, or boy, to handle.

I remembered my dad telling me about huge cattle drives with more than 50 cowhands and over 2,500 cattle, sometimes stretching two miles long. I heard stories about how some drives would start out with a thousand and arrive in Kansas with only half that number. I pledged to myself that I would not lose any of my longhorns. As I looked over the herd, I remembered when many of them were born. I remembered moving them from pasture to pasture, just the way my dad taught me. Hopefully, those lessons would do me well on this trip.

My dad. I imagined him on a cattle drive right now in Canada. I wondered if he was thinking about me right now. I wondered if he realized how lonely I would be and how much I missed him right now. One hundred forty-seven longhorns, me, Princess and Darlin'. Well, I figured we would do just fine.

There weren't many different trails from West Texas going to market – just one well-worn one. I knew I needed to travel east, toward the Chisholm Station, toward the Red River and the crossing. After that, I would head north through Oklahoma and then on in through Kansas to Abilene or Dodge City, whichever would give me the best price. Getting to the crossing would not be hard. The land was open and free, with many small creeks and rivers of fresh water for the herd, and long stretches of grassy plains. Once we reached the crossing, we would navigate the Red River. If you could get across the river when it was at a low point and not lose any longhorns there, you were doing great, but after that the problems started. Once I crossed the Red River, I would be in Oklahoma Territory. I remembered my dad talking about the long trail with little water and little grass to eat. Since so many cattle had already traversed this trail, and since I got such a late start, I supposed much of the food for my cattle would be gone. The grass would either be eaten down to bare ground or else trampled to nothingness. And the watering holes? They too, could be either empty, dried up, or just huge bowls of mud from too many herds and too much summer heat.

Well, there was not much I could do about that now.

So far, the ride has been calm and uneventful. The cattle were moving at a comfortable pace and I felt more confident every minute. As I looked at my herd, I remembered how fat and healthy they were. I had taken good care of them over the last year. I was pleased with how they looked. *They would make it, I thought to myself, and I will not lose a one.* Then I remembered again what else was on the way to Kansas. I would be in Indian Country. Some were friendly and some were not-so-friendly, as my dad would say. I had heard stories about how they would sometimes take a few head your cattle as a kind of payment for using their land. And if you were ornery toward them, they could cause you problems by chasing your herd off in all directions. That was the good part. The bad part would be running into those who would have little regard for human life.

But then, my dad always got along well with the Indians. He would tell stories how he taught them how to grow crops and to raise cattle. Often, he would bring back a blanket or moccasins or a pouch that some Indian chief would give my dad for helping them. Hopefully I could make it through without any problem.

It was nearing noon, or so I thought, but then I remembered my watch. I reached into my pocket and opened it up for the first time. Yes, I was right - eleven thirty on the dot. I was pleased I could tell the time even without a watch. Still, I was glad to have it. It must have been very special to my mom. I glanced inside the lid. It was a picture of my mom when she was little with her mother and my grandmother. I always felt Carrie looked like our mom, but to see her when she was Carrie's age; they looked almost the same. Now the watch was mine. It would be very special to me, too.

I was surprised how smooth the ride had been so far. Keeping the cattle rounded up had been a lot easier than I thought. They were mostly all gathered together by the time I had gotten to their grazing land. They knew me and would follow me close as I would move them from pastureland to pastureland. With a couple of yelps they seemed eager to move out and onto the trail. All appeared peaceful, and I felt comfortable so far, mainly because this was land I was familiar with from my other rides with my dad.

Once the evening had set in and the cattle were settled down, I would always tell my dad goodbye and head for home. Of course, we always would have supper before I left to go back. I liked sitting around the campfire and listening to my dad tell his tales. He knew how to make me laugh. He would make the stories so funny you would think I was in pain the way I would be crying from laughter and rolling around on the ground. *Supper tonight would not be the same and sitting by the fire would not be the same either,* I thought to myself.

Wait! I stood up in the saddle quickly, and then I slumped. No, it won't be the same. I forgot the matches! Mom did not pack them, because every time in the past, Dad had his own, and he carried them with him wherever he went. I never carried matches. All of a sudden, I had a real sinking feeling. Even in the heat of the middle of the day, I began to think about how cold the night would be. Without fire, I couldn't make coffee, or biscuits, or heat up the jerky I had brought.

As I was lost in my self-pity, I hadn't noticed that several of the cattle had decided to stray from the herd. I dropped the reins from Princess pointed her in the right direction and held on, pushing my heels hard into Darlin's side. She lunged forward, her hooves digging deep into the soil as she leaped into a gallop. She had chased many cows in the past, and she knew what to do. All I had to do was hold on tight as she cut them off and turned one, then another, back to the herd until all were safely together again.   During the chase, I had momentarily forgotten about not having any matches. I enjoyed chasing the cattle and feeling the wind in my face. I especially enjoyed the feel of Darlin' as I rode her. I could feel her strength, and her agility to make quick turns, yet never once was I afraid of being thrown off. Her golden-brown neck and flank glistened in the brightness of the afternoon sun. I listened to the thundering of her hooves as they pounded into the prairie soil. I could hear her breath as she snorted from the quick starts and sharp turns and when she finally stopped, I could hear her breathing heavy through her massive nostrils. I leaned over her head and put my arms around her as I ran one hand under her throat and the other along her neck and mane. Then all of a sudden, she became very still and quiet. I sensed she had seen something. I looked up and I found what she was looking at. Both of our eyes were staring straight ahead, at *him*.

There he was, on a ridge, directly ahead of us - standing proud and grand. The most beautiful white stallion I had ever seen. The wind on the ridge was blowing strong, picking up his tail and mane and blowing them straight out. He pawed the hard ground and kicked up small clouds of dust. He shook his head up and down. It was almost as if he were talking to me. It was as if I heard him say, *Yes, I will be yours, but you won't get me easy. You must want me with all your heart. And you must fight for me, and one day, I will be yours.*

With every stamp of his hooves and every nod of his head, his muscles rippled and shimmered. He knew he was the best, the strongest, the fastest who ever lived; and he knew that I knew it, too.

I could see why some thought he was a ghost. One minute you would see him and the next, he would be gone. If you were to look at him and rub your eyes to be sure of what you were seeing, he would be gone by the time you opened your eyes again.

And, yes, I guess Silas *was* right. He *was* like a streak of lightning. Fast, flashing and glimmering like shining silver, streaking across the hills and plains.

Yes, wild one, you will be mine one day, I said to myself. In a moment, he was gone, disappearing between the jagged rocks in the hills ahead. *And I will see you again, soon, my friend. Maybe not today, but I will be back.*

CHAPTER 14

A FRIEND COMES ALONG

Without matches, I thought I might as well eat a soda biscuit and a piece of jerky in the saddle, ride as long as I could, and settle the cattle in just before dark. Once it was dark, I wanted to get to sleep before it got too cool. I knew that if anything happened, Darlin' would wake me. I remembered the times Darlin' warned us when coyotes entered close to our livestock, or when rattlesnakes appeared near our campsites. If something were to happen out on the trail, I believed Darlin' would let us know.

I had not done too badly with my time. In fact, I was real proud of myself for getting as far as I had. Without having to stop to cook dinner, I was actually past the places I remembered stopping with my dad; like Five Forks Ravine where the five creeks all flowed to a deep gorge, just north of the trail, and Twin Peaks - two tall hills with the trail winding between them.

I had little time to be lonely, but, as the shadows stretched out in front of the herd, I began to feel a little lonesome. The cattle were tired, I could tell, or at least they were telling me they were tired as they began to slow when we reached a rise off the plains. I thought it would be a good place to stop. I guessed I was tired too, and so was Darlin'. My back and butt were sore from the long ride in the saddle, and I was sure Darlin' would be glad to get me off her back as well. We could not push them anymore, so I was glad the cattle finally decided to settle down on their own. I couldn't start a fire without matches, so I settled in the dark. The wind from the hills began to blow strong across us. I was glad my mom packed me several blankets, because I needed them.

Just as I had finally begun to rest, I heard the cattle stirring. Princess and Darlin' were also starting to snort and paw the ground. I heard a noise and I reached for my rifle. I lifted the barrel as I moved in the direction where I thought the noise was coming. I heard it again. Yes, there was something there, a mountain lion, perhaps, but what would he be doing out on the prairie? Could it be rustlers - cattle thieves? What would they want with just 147 head of cattle? We were too far from Indians, so it couldn't be them. I heard the noise again and this time I cocked my rifle. As I thought about having to pull the trigger, I suddenly remembered I had not loaded the gun. We never kept it loaded in the house, and I had not put any shells in the chamber since I left home. If it were mountain lions or rustlers or renegade

Indians, I couldn't shoot them; I would have to beat them to death with the stock of the rifle.

The night was not as bright as the night before. The moon was behind dark clouds in the sky. Even though I couldn't see, I knew something was there. Wait! It wasn't coming from the direction of the herd, but from behind me. I swung around and I saw a figure approach. I flipped the rifle, grabbed the barrel of it, and charged into the darkness toward the figure. As I raced forward, ready to battle, I raised the gun, intent on swinging it with all the power and strength I could muster. I let out a great yell, piercing the quiet of the night, and then I heard my name.

"Billy! It's me! Stop!" The figure blurted out.

I stopped dead in my tracks, but the rifle still held high in my hands, ready to swing.

"Who are you, and what do you want?" I screamed, still suspicious.

"It's me, Billy. Clark!"

Clark? Clark Turnipseed? That Clark?

Still amazed, I forced out his name, "Clark?" I got on one knee and lowered the rifle as I saw him, crouched down, huddled on the ground before me.

"Clark Turnipseed?" I repeated, "What are you doing here? It's really you?"

"Yes, it's me, Billy," gasped Clark, trying hard to catch his breath. "I thought you were going to kill me!"

Still startled that Clark would be here, I realized he was right. I yelled at him in the darkness, "You scared me to death! I never expected you to be here!" I panted, as I was also out of breath.

When we finally saw each other in the shadows as the moon gave us a glimmer of light, we began to laugh at the comedy that just unfolded.

Still laughing, I said, "I thought you were a mountain lion or a rustler or even an Indian! I might have killed you!"

"I didn't know if I had found you or not!" Clark puffed, "I thought you were going to shoot me dead, too!"

"I couldn't shoot you," I said.

"You couldn't? What do you mean?"

"I forgot to load my gun!"

With that, we both began to roll around with laughter that lasted several minutes. I was relieved that it was Clark and I did not have to face any outlaws or wild beasts. When we were finally able to speak again, I asked Clark one more time,

"What are you doing here? How did you find me? Why were you sneaking around out there? What were you...?"

Clark interrupted me, "Whoa! Billy! One question at a time!" He paused to take a deep breath. "Well, it started early this morning. I went by your house to thank you personally for what you did for me. I knew my father had seen you yesterday, but I was still feeling pretty groggy from that nasty bump on my head, and my mother, bless her soul, insisted that I not leave the house. When I arrived at your home this morning, you mother informed me that you had left, by yourself, on this cattle drive. I so much wanted to thank you, and I was terribly disappointed at not being able to express my gratitude for your heroics the night before. When I stopped by the bank to see my father, and tell him I had missed you, I couldn't believe what he said. First, he asked Charles if all the accounting was up-to-date and if he could handle the books for a couple of months on his own. When Charles replied in the affirmative, he turned to me and said, 'Clark, I think you owe that young man a lot. I'm going to excuse you to go and help him with that cattle rounding thing.'

"I told him, 'It's a cattle drive, father.' He laughed and told me to go home, pack and find you, and that is how I got here."

I was amazed and happy all at the same time. I watched Clark as he sat and pulled his knees toward his chest and wrapped his arms tightly around his legs.

"Are you cold? I'm sorry," I apologized, "I don't have a fire. I forgot to get matches before I left."

"Oh, I forgot to tell you. I went by your mother's to tell her what I was going to do, and she handed these to me." Clark reached into his coat pocket and took out a tin, packed with matches inside. "She said you probably needed these. Oh, and she also told me to remind you that you need to load your gun because you might need it." Clark tried to keep a straight face, but he couldn't hold it as he burst into laughter again, and I quickly joined him in the fun.

Within a few minutes, I had a small fire burning and we sat close to the flames to keep warm. Maybe my mom knew I would be having company on the trail. She packed enough food for two, maybe three people.

"And there is one more thing," said Clark, "Mr. Jacobs gave me a letter for you. It is from your dad. It came just this morning."

I swiftly reached for it and I read it in the light of the fire.

Dear Billy,

I usually write to your mom, but since you are the one heading up this drive, I wanted to write it to you. If you are grown up enough to take cattle to market, you are grown up enough to get your own letters. I meant to tell you in the last letter where you will need to go on the drive. I have friends who will be meeting you at the crossing. They have orders to pay you for your cattle at a good price and take them the rest of the way to Kansas. This way, you don't have to cross into the Oklahoma Territory and face the Indian nation. I know the Indians have all been friendly to me, but I don't want you to have any problems. By selling your longhorns to a bigger herd, there is a better chance of them making it without any problems. Once you sell your herd, you can head on back home to take care of your mom. It is strange, son, that I am here on the biggest cattle drive of my life and you are there doing the same thing. I think about you often, and pray the best for you.

Love,

Dad

PS By the way, you want to ask for Captain Watson. He's the trail boss.

I read the letter several times before I put it down.

"Good news, I hope, Billy?" Clark asked.

I smiled and said, "Yes, good news." I took a deep breath, "I am so glad you're here Clark. Thanks for coming and bringing me this letter and thanks for being willing to help."

"I owe you a lot, Billy," Clark whispered.

I didn't remark about that, but I added, "Well it's getting very late and we have a long day ahead of us. We will talk more in the morning."

Clark nodded in agreement and in the next few minutes, we prepared our bedrolls and were soon ready for sleep. For a moment, I felt very content. The letter was from my dad to me - just to me! And he was thinking about me. He knew I would be on the trail, just like him! That night I fell asleep feeling very happy.

CHAPTER 15

HEADING ACROSS TEXAS

The next morning I woke up early. When I pulled the blanket from over my face, I was surprised to see Clark up already. He did not notice me, but I could see him working on starting the fire, and he was not having any luck. I covered my head again and stretched under the covers and made a loud noise like I was yawning. When I sat up, I noticed Clark had jumped up and was putting his bedroll on his horse.

"Good morning," I bellowed in a deeper-than-usual voice, "How did you sleep?"

"Oh, fine," Clark answered. "Well, not really. That ground is a lot harder than anything I've ever slept on, but I'll get used to it."

It looked like he didn't get any sleep at all. His eyes were puffy, his hair was a mess, and his clothes were wrinkled and dirty. He must have tossed and turned all night.

"I thought you might like some breakfast," he remarked, "so I gathered some wood. I was just going to get some more. You want to get the fire going while I find more wood?"

"Sure," I replied, as I moved to the stack of wood he had left for me. I noticed that he did not have enough kindling to get it started. So, while he was away, I took out my knife and began to shave some small slivers into a pile. When I had enough, I placed it near a rock to block the wind from blowing it out before it even got started. As the flame began to grow, I added more of the wood slivers and then some of the twigs and then branches I had broken off the wood Clark had already gathered. By the time he had returned, I had a nice fire going. I had rolled two of the larger logs together on either side of the fire to protect it from the wind and to balance our coffee pot and skillet for cooking.

"Hey, that's great!" he remarked. "I was going to start it, but I didn't think we had enough wood yet. I was going to bring some food, but your mother told me that she had packed enough for us for most of the trip."

"Yeah, we have plenty. Do you want to make the biscuits?" I had gotten the skillet out and had pulled off a wad of lard to put in the skillet and set it across the two logs. The lard began to sizzle immediately. I reached for the canteen, a cup, and the bag of flour and tossed them to Clark and they landed at his feet.

I turned back around to get the coffee, the pot and two more cups. I had a pretty good idea he had never made biscuits before, at least not out on the prairie. My mom had made some sourdough biscuits for us to eat, but, rather than eating them now, I was saving them for the trail - to eat while we rode. Right now, I was enjoying the reaction of Clark to all this outdoor cooking activity. I realized he probably had never spent much time fending for himself. As I turned around with the coffee, I began to feel badly for him.

"You know," I said with a real concerned look on my face, "I'm quite picky 'bout my biscuits. If they're not just like my mom's, I get real annoyed like, so maybe I better make those biscuits this morning. You don't mind, do you?" I could hardly contain my laughter. I had to turn away so Clark could not see the grin I had on my face.

"Oh, of course, go right ahead," he agreed eagerly. "A man's got to do what a man's got to do. Right?"

He seemed relieved not to have to make the biscuits. I poured some flour and salt into the cup, added a little water and mixed it with my knife. Once it was thick and sticky, I scooped out a spoonful and dropped it into the skillet. I had enough to make four biscuits, and while they were cooking, I had the coffee made in a short time. Clark was still staring at the skillet with the biscuits I had just made. He did not look too hungry. In fact, he looked downright sickly. I handed him his cup and poured the coffee in it. I reached for the sugar and offered some to him. That snapped him out of his daze about the biscuits, and he took the bag of sugar. He began to look around, I think, for a spoon. He did not say a thing, but then finally reached into the bag and took out a pinch of sugar and dropped it into his cup. I took my knife and flipped the biscuits over and they had become a golden brown. I sat near the fire and I could feel the warmth. It had been cool that morning, but I could tell that the day would become very hot. As I sipped my coffee, Clark sat down near me.

"You do this often?" he said.

"Do what?"

"Eat outside."

I thought I would tease him a bit. "Oh, 'bout as often as I can." I stretched my neck up as if I was surveying the land, and added, "Maybe we can shoot us a prairie dog this morning and we can gut'm and skin'm and have some meat with these biscuits."

With that, Clark dropped his coffee and headed about twenty feet away and fell to his knees. He was sick. I didn't mean to make him sick. Now, I felt bad for sure. In a couple of minutes, he was back, wiping his mouth with his handkerchief.

I just then noticed his clothes again. He had the fanciest shoes I have ever seen anyone wear on a cattle drive. He had these short pants with his stockings showing. He had a little jacket that only covered to his waist. I realized he had not been prepared for this trip. For one thing, those shoes would not last for long. They were not made for walking across rocks or wading into the creeks and rivers. And those pants. They were almost comical. When we would get to brush country, his legs and those stockings will be torn to pieces. With that little, thin coat, he must have been real cold last night. Maybe that's why he couldn't sleep. Clark was about my size, even though he was about eight or nine years older than me. I knew I was not real big for my age, but Clark was small, I thought, for a man his age. His blond hair was really a mess this morning. I remembered meeting him at the Turnipseed's the first day I was at their house. His hair was neat and oiled down then. Now, it was all messy with bits of leaves and grass stuck to it. His face was fair in color, much more than his brother Charles. Clark was more like his sister, Samantha.

Samantha. I had not thought of her much since I was at her house. Now that Clark was here, I could find out more about her. But, we had plenty of time for that. This would be a long trip.

"Are you alright?" I questioned, hiding my laughter.

"Yes, I'll be fine. I have to confess, I am not an outdoorsman. The thought of eating a wild animal from this range made me feel a little queasy." He must have noticed me looking over his clothes. "I don't assume I am properly dressed for a trail ride, am I?" He said with a sheepish grin on his face.

"I fancy that once we get to brush country, those short pants of yours aren't going to be much protection on your legs," I replied, now with a little more sympathy in my voice. "But," I continued, "we'll fix up something. Maybe we will pick up some pants at the trading post at the Crossing. You'll do all right. Why, once this trip is done, you'll become a bonafide cowhand for sure!"

I remembered I had worn Clark's clothes when I first visited Samantha and fell into the lemonade. We were the same size, but on this trip, I didn't think about bringing extra clothes. If I had, I could have loaned them to Clark. He could have used them.

With that encouragement, he seemed to perk up, and, from that moment on, he was full of questions - always asking what this tree is called, how do you brand the cows and did it hurt, how do you teach a horse to cut cattle. At the end of the day, I was not sure if I was more tired from herding cattle or answering all of Clark's questions.

The good news was that I had someone to trail with me. I enjoyed the company and Clark was learning quickly how to help with the longhorns. I figured we were still making about ten miles a day. If we could keep it up, we would be at the Red River in three, maybe four weeks. If I could meet up with the other herds at the crossing, and I could sell my stock, we would easily be back home within two months.

CHAPTER 16

A CHANGE OF WEATHER ON THE TRAIL

We had been on the trail for over a week and so far, the weather had been typical for West Texas - hot and dry. Since the time we had left Ringgold, the skies had been clear with only hints of tiny strands of clouds overhead. But today, things were different. Those clouds, which were only a wisp the day before, had become dark and heavy with rain. The wind had picked up, and I noticed the herd had sensed the change in the weather as well. As the day wore on, the sky became bleaker and darker, and the cattle became more and more agitated. Even Darlin' was acting a bit skittish.

"I think we are in for a fierce downpour," I hollered out to Clark.

"Yes," he agreed, "it seems we are going to have a bit of precipitation."

Pre-cip-i-ta-tion? I guessed that was an Eastern word for rain. Why didn't he just say *rain?*

"Right," I added, "we better gather in the herd and try to keep them huddled together. If it comes to lightning and thundering, I want to be able to control them and not let them get spooked."

"I'm on it!" shouted Clark as he raced to get ahead of the herd.

As he went to the left, I broke to the right. Since we were pretty much on the open range, it did not provide many places to drive the longhorns for protection or for control. As I watched Clark, I could see a narrow ridge and a small ravine up ahead and to the left of the herd. I waved to Clark to lead the cattle toward it. He nodded in agreement and went right to work on it. I thought we could keep the cattle there until this blew over. As we got closer to the ridge, I could see ahead of Clark. I hadn't noticed it before, but the sky right beyond the ridge was now almost black, and I could see in the near distance that the rain had already begun.

In a week, Clark had learned a lot about herding, camping on the trail and was doing a good job of leading the cattle, however, I realized that we would not get them there before the heavens opened and we would be in the midst of a mighty powerful storm.

As the rains began and the hard pellets of water started to beat down upon us, Clark worked earnestly to get the cattle to the cover and the protection of the ridge. Soon the cattle were moving to group themselves against the ridge, trying to avoid the rain that was now coming down in sheets. In no time at all, the drizzle became so heavy it blurred my vision.

The ground was becoming soaked. It was starting to become difficult for Darlin' to walk through the mud much less against the driving downpour. I decided to dismount and help Darlin' wade through the mud that was now covering the ground, which only moments before was dry and dusty. My boots began to slide and I was losing my balance. I now needed Darlin' to help me stay standing. I had been walking with my head down to keep the rain out of my face. I tried looking up, but every time I raised my head, the drops would sting my face and eyes under my hat.

I could not hear the longhorns and I tried yelling out for Clark. With the thunder and roar of the storm, I'm sure he could not hear me, and I could hear nothing else. I must have lost track of my direction. My boots were now completely under water. I thought it was strange, since the ridge would offer a place that would be higher and would not flood. I was wrong.

Without warning, I felt the water begin to rise quickly. I must have wandered too far away from the ridge, and I was headed for the ravine below it. As I watched the water rise around me, I suddenly heard a roar that brought fear to my heart. A wall of water all of a sudden crashed against me, causing me to lose my footing. I still had the reins to Darlin' in my hand but, at the same time the water forced me off my feet, the reins slid out of my hand. I was now at the mercy of the deluge of water that was sweeping me along the ravine.

My body began to tumble, and I could not gain my balance. The ground below, although softened and muddy by the rain, now felt like sharp rocks against my legs, arms, stomach, and back as I was twirled and twisted along. The surging water was washing me away. I felt like I was going to drown as I struggled to raise my head to gasp for breaths of air. I tried to rub the water out of my eyes so I could see where I was going. As I peered through the rushing waves around me, the last thing I remembered was seeing an enormous boulder right before me.

"Billy, are you hurt? Billy, speak to me! Billy!" It was dark, but I could hear someone talking to me. *Where am I? What happened? What's going on? Who's calling my name?* I felt a cloth rubbing my forehead, and it hurt. My body winced at the pain.

"You're alive! Thank God! I thought you were lost for sure!"

I heard the voice again, but as I tried to force my eyes open, my eyelids felt as if they were glued shut. I struggled to sit up, but I felt a hand push me back down.

"You are in no shape to be getting up quite yet," the voice said.

With that, I let my body slump back down. As I did, I began to feel pain, not only on my head, but also all over - my back, my legs and arms and across my chest. When I finally allowed my body to relax, my mind slowly began to recollect what had happened to me. My first thoughts were about water rushing all around and over me. I remembered how this forceful, streaming flood was tossing my body and how I was trying to breathe but only getting mouthfuls of gritty water. Then in a flash, I remembered the cattle, and Darlin' and - and Clark. My body lurched upward, and I felt what must have been Clark's hands grabbing my arms.

"Hold on there! Take it easy!"

He pushed me back down. He must have sensed my confusion, and he began to reassure me.

"Everything is fine. The cattle are fine, and Darlin's right here with me."

Trying to sit upright made my head pound even harder. I took a deep breath and sighed, as I forced out the words, "Clark, is that you? Are you all right? What happened to me? Where are we? Are the cattle safe? The storm! Is it over?"

"Hey, believe me, everything is fine. You got caught up in a flash flood and were swept away. You must have hit your head on a rock or something. You have a big cut on your head and probably bled a lot. That's why you seem so weak. You have some cuts and scratches all over, but don't worry. Even though everything maybe a little wet, we are all alive and safe. With a little rest, I think you are going to be just fine."

The more I listened to Clark, the clearer my thoughts became. Yes, I began to remember the sudden storm, and the driving rain. I remembered trying to gather the longhorns near a ridge for protection. I remembered the gushing water and being dragged along with the flood. I remember seeing a boulder and - well, that was the last thing I remembered until I heard Clark's voice.

The whole time I was talking I could feel Clark wiping my face and my eyes with a wet cloth.

"You had a lot of blood in your eyes," he said, answering my question before I even asked it. "There," he continued, "try opening your eyes now."

I did not know what to expect when I opened my eyes. *Is it still daylight? Is the storm gone? Is it still flooded?* I put my hands to my eyes and rubbed them as if I had been sleeping forever. I raised my eyelids slightly and saw that, yes, it was still day. I blinked several times, and then I stretched my eyes as wide open as I could. The first thing I saw was a grinning Clark. He had a smile that went from ear to ear. I studied his face, and he seemed to have a look of relief. I leaned up on one elbow and I used the other hand to touch a bandage wrapped across the front of my head. When I felt my head, I sent a shiver of pain throughout my body.

"Don't touch that! It is starting to heal over and you don't need to lose any more blood," Clark said.

"Where did you get a bandage?" I asked.

Clark pulled off his jacket and I could see one of his sleeves was missing. He smiled and put his jacket back on.

I felt like I had been in a fight with Thomas and he had pummeled me to death's door. I was sore in every part of my body. Every time I tried to move a muscle, it hurt. When I realized that everything was safe, I slowly laid back down. I closed my eyes and I fell asleep.

"Good morning, sleepyhead! Are you ready to rise and shine?" It was Clark's voice.

I was thinking about sitting up, but I remembered how my head hurt when

I tried it earlier. This time I moved slower, but, to my surprise, much of the pain I felt before had eased. I felt rested and more alert.

"Wow! That was a gully washer! Seems like it must have been a short storm though." I slowly opened my eyes, squinting against the brightness of the day. "The sky is already clear," I said, as I moved my head to look all around me, "Not a cloud in the sky."

"Well, you are right about one thing," I heard Clark say, "it was a short storm, but the sky didn't really clear up until today."

"What do you mean, *today?*"

Clark looked at me square in the eyes and said, "Billy, the storm was two days ago!"

"Two da-," I screeched as I began to lunge forward. I quickly stopped as I felt the pain in other parts of my body. In a much softer, calmer voice I said, "Two days? I've been here two days?"

"It was almost nightfall before I finally found you!" Clark's voice had a slight tremor, and I could see in his face that he was worried about me.

"Actually, it was Darlin' I found first. When I got up close enough to her, I saw that she was standing over you." We both turned and looked at Darlin' as she was grazing nearby, oblivious to our stares. "If she had not been with you, I might not have ever found you and you could have died out here."

Clark looked away as his voice started to crack, and for a moment, I thought he might have started crying.

"Well, Clark, I guess you paid me back, right?" I waited for him to answer.

"It's just that –", he started to speak but he turned quickly to the fire and jumped up to go to it, "The biscuits! They're burning!"

Without thinking, he tried to grab the skillet, but it burned his hand and he dropped it quickly. The skillet hit the ground, and we watched the biscuits flop neatly into the fire. Clark grabbed a stick near the fire and used it to reach in under them and toss them out of the fire. For a brief moment, we thought he had saved the biscuits only to watch them land in a muddy puddle a few feet away. Both of us had a dead glaze to our eyes as we watched the biscuits slowly suck up the dirty water in that puddle. At the same time, we both started to chuckle and the laughter grew until it made my head hurt worse than ever.

Clark and I continued to talk about the storm, and I was sad to hear that we had lost two of the cattle. I wanted to go and look for them right away. It would always make me sad when one of our cattle would die on the trail or drift off where we couldn't find it. I knew they could not survive out here, or at least I thought they couldn't make it without me. I hoped they would be alright. Maybe someone would find them and take them to another herd. Whatever happened to them, it still made me very sad.

Clark insisted we stay longer at the campsite, but I was too antsy to just sit and rest. I needed to be back on the trail. I convinced Clark I was fine, and my persistence worked. He let me climb on Darlin', but he made sure we took a slow pace. I agreed.

Having lost two days on the trail, I felt we were behind schedule, but right now, taking it slowly seemed to be the best idea.

I never mentioned it again, but I knew Clark had saved my life. *Wait until we get back to Ringgold*, I thought to myself. *The Sheriff and Mr. Turnipseed will be calling Clark a hero, too.*

CHAPTER 17

HEADING FOR THE CROSSING

I had never been to the crossing. I remembered my dad talking about it though. He had told me the story many times about how he could see it from miles away because of the dust cloud stirred up by all the cattle. He said there would be thousands of longhorns coming from all over Texas - south, west and east - being herded to that one place to cross the Red River. He said you couldn't miss it. Once he hit the Red River as he drove the cattle east, he just followed the bank until he found a great bend in the river. There would be the crossing. I would be doing the same thing.

The land would flatten out and my dad said sandbars could be seen poking out like pig's backs in a mud hole. It was an easy place for the longhorns to cross, and if the water was not too high, they could just walk across with no problem. But, if it was high, they had to swim and then you had to be very careful not to lose any. I figured, this late in the season, the high water from the melted snow would be gone and the water wouldn't be high at all. My dad had told stories about having to rescue cowhands who lost their grip and fell in or got swept off their horses. I remembered a story someone told me about my dad when three of the cowhands got caught up in a whirlpool and got sucked under. They told how my dad threw a lasso and let it settle to the bottom and then, yanking with all his might, he roped all three at the same time and pulled them to safety. I was ready to tell that story to Clark, but I decided not to. Too many times I told stories about my dad, and folks made fun of me. He had not asked me much about the 'legendary Bill Pecos'. Maybe he felt like Samantha did. She seemed to understand that having a rich dad was about how I felt with having a famous dad. Maybe Clark understood that, too, and that was the reason he hadn't said much to me about him.

We had been riding for about two weeks, and we had not seen one other cattle drive. I kept looking for the cloud of dust but I didn't see it. I started to think that maybe the friends of my dad were not going to be there waiting for us. Finally we reached the Red River and we let the herd water. I knew this was not the crossing yet - the water was too fast, and there was no great bend in the river, and the banks were too steep for the cattle to climb. I was beginning to get nervous, and I wasn't sure what to do.

Clark had become somewhat of an expert with the cattle. His horse was called Brownie, and I had ridden her often to help teach her to cut cattle. She was not a natural like Darlin', but she was learning enough to help with the drive. While Clark was riding my horse, he was learning how to stay on when a horse decides to get to work cutting cattle. He had a few near spills, but had managed to hang on. Now he and Brownie were working together as a team, and it was good to see someone so eager to learn and help. He had even learned to make biscuits and coffee on the trail and to get a fire going in almost no time.

We had not quite gotten the herd ready to drive one morning, when Clark saw something.

"Billy, are those riders?" he said as he squinted, looking off into the early morning sun. I jumped up from putting out the morning fire and, squinting too, I saw them.

"Yes! They are!" I shouted, and I immediately threw my saddle on Darlin'. "I'm going to talk to them. Wait here with the herd. I'll be right back!"

I mounted Darlin' and we galloped off in a flash. Maybe they had news about the crossing or about the trail riders I was supposed to meet. I was still a long distance off from them when they must have seen the cloud of dust I was kicking up as I raced toward them. They stopped and turned to face me. I could count four of them. As I got closer, I could see their faces. They looked very tired and they had full beards that covered their brown, wrinkled faces. Their clothes were covered with dust and there was no color to anything they wore. From the smell, it was obvious they had not bathed in a long time.

As I pulled up to face them, they were all lined up side by side, each with an arm across his body, leaning on his saddle horn.

"Howdy," I said in as friendly a tone as I could gather within me. I waited for a response but none was offered, so I continued.

"I'm here to meet up with a cattle drive."

There was still no response nor even the slightest movement from any one of them. I was starting to become a little nervous. I took a deep breath, and I broke the silence again.

"I'm here to meet Captain Watson."

With that proclamation, they all began to sit up and adjust themselves in their saddles, and looked back and forth at each other. The one in the middle grabbed his saddle horn with both hands, leaned across the neck of his horse and instead of a spoken word, he rolled his lips around and spat a wad of tobacco right in front of me. With that, the men began to chuckle, but it does not ease my fear. Finally, one of the other men started to talk.

"Cap'n Watson ain't here," he said as I sat and waited for what seemed a long time for him to continue.

I wanted to ask many questions but I was afraid of not getting too many answers.

"He crossed over a week, week and a half ago," he said, but another interrupted and spoke with a voice so deep, it sounded like he was speaking from a well,

"Nearer to three week, I recollect."

"Ya missed him, sonny," interjected another with a much higher voice, which sounded almost shrill.

Now that I was close enough to see them better, none of them seemed much older than Clark, but they looked worn and beaten.

"Well, my dad says I need to find him," I said as I began to turn my horse to head back to my herd.

"Yer daddy, boy?" one said and with that they all began to laugh.

"Good luck," I heard one of them say.

I started to turn my horse back around, but the men seemed to relax a little, and they began to talk more openly to me.

"Look, fella. We just left Cap'n Watson. We're the lucky ones. We got out alive. We was in an ambush by the Indians, and we was in a standoff. We escaped, but the others - they may be all kilt off by now."

Another offered his view, "All you gonna find is blood and bones, if'n the buzzards and coyotes ain't et'm already."

The deep voiced one said, as he pulled his horse back and started to head away, "We got away, and we ain't goin' back."

As I sat there on Darlin', and watched the others follow the deep-voiced one and slowly amble away, my heart began to sink. I wanted to blame someone for what had happened, but I couldn't think of anyone. I wanted to be mad at someone, but who? My dad, for not being here? The postal rider for getting that first letter to us so late? Captain Watson for not waiting? Those cowardly cowhands for running from a fight? Myself? Now was not the time to wallow in my own pity. I knew what I had to do. I had to take the cattle myself. I started to yell back at the four. I wanted to ask about the crossing, but I guessed they hadn't been in that direction. I could find it myself. We would just keep heading east along the river. I knew we would find it. Now, I had to tell Clark the news. What would he say? Would he too turn tail and run? Would he be willing to cross with me? Would he be willing to head into Indian Country, knowing what had happened there? I couldn't lie to him. I had to tell him the truth, or at least, what those riders told me to be the 'truth'.

Many thoughts were going through my mind as I rode back to our camp, much slower than I had ridden off. *What would my dad do*, I thought? I put myself in his shoes, and I believed he would press on. With that resolve, I picked up the trot and Darlin' and I headed back with renewed desire to carry on. As I got closer to the herd, I noticed a wagon was now stopped at our camp, and I saw Clark and another man talking with each other. Clark saw me approach and said to me, "Billy, I hope those gentlemen were as helpful to you as this fine gentleman was to me."

"Yes," I replied, "somewhat," not wanting to divulge too much of what I heard in front of this stranger, "I learned a few things about what is up ahead."

After my encounter with the four foul-smelling, cowardly dirt-bags, I was not too trusting of anyone else I would meet on this trail.

"Well, Billy, this fellow has been a wealth of information," Clark said as if he had all the answers to my problems. "Let me introduce to you to Mr. Chisholm. Mr. Chisholm, this is my good friend, Billy."

Neither of us offered a handshake, but we nodded a welcome to each other. I was glad Clark did not mention who my dad was. I'd learned to be very caution around new people, and I didn't trust anyone until I knew them better and that included this stranger.

Mr. Chisholm began to tell me what he and Clark were discussing. "Well, young man, you missed Captain Watson. He crossed over almost two weeks ago." I knew that much from those hooligans, but he continued. "Seems he met with a hostile group of Indians and there has been a standoff about a week's ride into the Indian Country."

That was something I already knew too. It did not seem as if Mr. Chisholm was going to tell me anything I wasn't aware of already, but then he added,

"Those Indians were as mad as hornets ever since about four drunken cowboys rode through their village and knocked over several of their houses and ran off with some of their horses. They weren't part of Captain Watson's cowhands, but so far, the Captain has not been able to persuade the Indians of that. And the Chief wants those hoodlums himself!"

"Billy, the gents you just spoke with; could they have been those cowboys?" Clark questioned.

"Oh, I don't know, Clark. I don't know," I replied. I didn't want to give too much information to this man until I knew him better. Those four were probably the scoundrels Mr. Chisholm was talking about. I should have known. They lied to me!

Then Mr. Chisholm offered some advice. "I'd be very careful about taking your cattle to meet up with the Captain, young man. Those Indians are not happy now, and I'm not sure what can be done to ease that situation."

"Thank you, sir. I appreciate what you said, but we've not seen the crossing. Do you know where it is?" I asked.

"Do I? Yes indeed. I own the general store that sits on its bank. I am on my way there after picking up a few supplies for the cowhands who will be venturing back to Texas soon. If you are ready to ride, I'll trail along with you and get you there. It's just around that soft ridge to your left about 3 more miles."

As we continued, I began to feel very confident. I looked over at Clark and he did not seem to be afraid to head into Indian Country. Maybe he was fooling me. Maybe he was not so brave on the inside. I was worried about nothing. All of a sudden, I felt like I could do anything, be anything, and go anywhere. I was Bill Pecos' son and I was proud of that.

It did not take long before we were near the crossing. I did not know what to expect, but it was just like my dad described it - a wide, flat part of the river in a big sweeping bend with slow moving water and sandbars, dotted across the middle. The other side was flat, too, and that would make it easy for the cattle to cross. The crossing store was called Red River Station and was not as big as I expected. It had a small porch and a very sturdy fence around it, and several hitching posts in front of that. There were several large fenced corrals to hold the cattle before they were herded across the river. Mr. Chisholm jumped out of his wagon and opened one of the holding pens, and we guided our longhorns in. It appeared Mr. Chisholm wanted us to stop, and he motioned for us to follow him into the store. Once inside, it was difficult to walk around the store because of all the supplies piled up along the walls. There were barrels of feed and flour, and huge sacks of corn and oats stacked almost to the ceiling. There were pots and pans and cups and ladles hanging so low from the ceiling, even I had to duck to miss hitting my head. The shelves were full of canned beans and peaches lining the walls. There were huge glass bowls of chewing and smoking tobacco on the counter as well as hard rock candy and containers of boiled eggs soaking in vinegar. There were long strips of jerky and cans of molasses, and a barrel of pickles. We must have looked hungry as we gawked at all the food surrounding us.

"Well, boys, I bet you are a mite hungry, am I right?" we heard Mr. Chisholm say.

"Well, to be plain truthful, sir, we have been eating jerky and skillet biscuits since we left home, and right about now, we—" Mr. Chisholm cut me off as I was about to confess we were getting low on a few of our supplies. We probably would not have enough to get us to Captain Watson and back home again.

"Well, son," he said, as he handed me an envelope, "Right before Captain Watson took off, he left this for you."

I was surprised that he knew me. "How do you know it's for me?" I asked.

"You *are* Bill Pecos' son, aren't you?" he replied. "The Captain had been waiting for you and since you were the only drive asking about him, I figured it had to be you."

"Do you know my dad?"

"Oh, yes, I know him and my dad knew him, too – a lot better than me."

As I opened the letter, out fell a five-dollar gold piece. It hit the floor, but Clark was there to scoop it up quickly. The letter said,

Dear Young Bill,

I could not wait any longer. I needed to get my herd moving. I hope you have made it this far. If you did, then Mr. Chisholm will help you find me, and I hope you can move fast enough to catch up with me. The money is to help you buy any supplies you may need. Just remember I will take the five dollars out of the money I will pay you for your longhorns.

Sincerely,

Captain John J. Watson

Five dollars. That would buy enough supplies. As I looked up from the letter, I saw Mr. Chisholm stacking some small bags of flour, salt and coffee and a tin of lard, onto the counter and pulling cans of beans and peaches off his shelves. I saw him reach in and take out a large hand of rock candy and a big slab of taffy. As I looked over the provisions, I asked Mr. Chisholm, "Do we have enough left over to buy a canteen? We need an extra." Clark and I had been sharing one since we joined up.

"That's not a problem," he answered, "you'll have enough."

"Well, if that's true and you know we will be coming back this way, and you know I will be getting the money for my herd, do you think you can sell us a pair of boots for Clark and maybe a pair of pants too? And a jacket? I will pay the balance as soon as we return."

Clark looked up when I mentioned his name, and glanced back down at his shoes and trousers. His shoes were about done - not much left of them. And the trousers? They were well worn, and on his legs, where the pants did not cover, were streaks of fresh and dried blood from cuts by thorns and bushes.

"I believe we can take care of that and a lot more too," Mr. Chisholm said, sizing Clark up for boots and pants. It did not take Clark long to find what he wanted. He took the first pair of boots and pants he tried on. Then Mr. Chisholm reached behind a glass door and pulled out a big white hat and handed it to Clark. He tried it on and turned to stare at himself in a looking glass. It was a perfect fit. Judging by the grin on Clark's face, I think he was very pleased.

"Thank you, Billy. Thank you, Mr. Chisholm. I will pay you both back as soon as I can. Now I feel like a real cowboy." Still staring at himself, he then let out a loud,

"Y-i-i-i-i-h-a-a-a!" that had both Mr. Chisholm and me laughing. I turned to Mr. Chisholm and said, "Thank you sir. I appreciate what you did."

"No, Billy, don't thank me. It's me who needs to thank you, or better yet, your dad," he said.

"What do you mean?" I asked.

"Well, I hear tell, a long time ago, this crossing was just another worthless piece of land until your dad came through with what was called the largest herd anyone had ever heard of. Do you think it was always flat like this?"

Before I could respond, he answered himself.

"No, it wasn't. It was much too steep and the water ran too fast. A lot of cattle drives lost a lot of longhorns up and down the Red River because the cattle drivers could not find a safe place for the cattle to cross. But that did not stop your dad. No, sir. Now, the story I heard was that he ran that herd along the banks, back and forth, back and forth, until he had created a great bend in the river, and at the same time, those longhorns had leveled out the banks on both sides. It was the most amazing thing I could ever imagine. I was told that this little station was barely able to keep the former owners in business. But, once those longhorns could navigate the river, every herd since then has used the Red River Crossing as a safe place to get their cattle from Texas to Kansas. So, you see, I am where I am today because of your dad. Soon after, my dad took over, and that is why I am thanking you."

By this time, Clark had joined us and was listening to the tale. Just as Mr. Chisholm finished his story, the front door opened. The bright sunlight filled the small store, and was blinding the first few moments. Mr. Chisholm left us and moved to the front to see what the visitors wanted. I tried to shade my eyes from the sun as it was setting and streaking into the shop. As I did so, I saw four figures enter the building. In a flash, I realized these were the four I had met earlier in the day. I did not want them to see me, so I crouched behind a stack of blankets.

Clark, with a puzzled look on his face, leaned over and asked, "What's going on?"

"Try to get Mr. Chisholm to come over here and don't mention me to those men."

"What?"

"Just do it. I will explain later."

In a moment, Mr. Chisholm had joined me and I asked him, "Were those men with Captain Watson when he was here?"

"No," he answered, "Why?"

"I think they are the men who were drunk and stole the Indians' horses. I met them on the trail right before I met you."

"I know this," he said.

"They said they were with Captain Watson and had escaped the attack. I don't believe them. I think they lied about that."

"You know what, I believe you. They had stopped here while Captain

Watson was waiting for you and I remember they left right before he did. And those were not the horses they were riding then. We must think of a way to capture them. Let me get back to them before they get suspicious."

"Wait!" I whispered, "I have a plan. You will know what to do. Just be ready."

Mr. Chisholm nodded in agreement and returned to the four.

Now, Clark came close beside me and asked, "What's going on?"

"Those four men are the ones who riled up the Indians. We can't let them leave here."

Clark and I looked at each other, and we knew what we needed to do. I motioned I would go out the back door. He pointed to a rope hanging near the counter. I smiled and headed out the back while he got the rope and headed out the front. I ran around to the front and Clark was already standing there. He tossed me an end to the rope and we tied it tightly around the fence posts on either side of the store front.

Once secure, Clark yelled out in as deep a voice as he could, "Hey, look, Indians are heading here from across the river! And they look mad!"

Almost before he could get it all out, the front door flew open and the four misfits bolted out of the store, in full run, heading for their horses. But before they could reach them, each one of the four caught his foot on the rope and fell, sprawling themselves across the dirt below. No sooner had they hit the ground, than Mr. Chisholm was standing over them with his shotgun, cocked and ready to fire.

"Excellent work boys," he bellowed, proud to be a part of a capture of these thieves. "Alright you low life, good-for-nothing, worthless sidewinders, undo your belts and drop those guns, and don't think of trying anything unless you want a new hole through you!"

Mr. Chisholm looked real proud of himself as he stood there with that big barrel shotgun, grinning from ear to ear.

We quickly tied up the four and latched them to the front hitching posts.

"Well, boys," Mr. Chisholm roared, "I will take care of these four. You take off like the wind for Captain Watson."

We hesitated, but he swung that big barrel up and pointed it across the river. "Now, get going, and don't dally." With that, we loaded our supplies, jumped on our horses, gathered our cattle and took off across the Red River into Indian Country.

CHAPTER 18

MEETING UP WITH A STRANGER

I had never been far from West Texas in my life, and now I was galloping across the Oklahoma Territory. So far it was not much different than West Texas, except the hills were starting to roll a little higher and a little longer.

We were almost a week from the Crossing when we noticed a cloud of dust trailing behind us. It was a lone rider and he was traveling fast. Clark and I got a little worried that it might be one of the outlaws who we captured back at the Crossing. We decided to split up, with Clark continuing forward with the herd, and I would circle back and try to get behind the rider. At the rate he was going, he would get to us within the hour.

As soon as we had topped a hill, Clark lit out straight ahead and I headed full speed west to wait and watch and circle back behind him. It didn't take long for the rider to catch up with Clark. I was sure not to make a sound or to kick up any dust to let him know he was being followed. I slowly took out my rifle, and this time I made sure it was loaded. As I watched from the distance, creeping closer and closer, I could see he had caught up to Clark and they had both dismounted. They were standing in front of their horses near a clump of short prairie bushes. I dismounted too and was about fifty yards away as I sneaked behind them. After creeping along the ground and, now, only about fifteen yards from them, I raised my rifle. Walking quickly toward them, I aimed it directly at the stranger.

"Don't move, mister, I'm a good shot, and if you as much as twitch, then you're a goner!" I yelled through clenched teeth.

"Wait! Billy! This is the Deputy Marshal! Don't shoot!" yelled back Clark.

My eyes must have been as big as saucers and a big lump was in my throat that made it was hard to swallow. It was even a bigger surprise when the stranger turned around. He was a black man! I had never seen one this close before. His skin was very dark; darker than that black mare Mr. Ledbetter had in his stable. As I looked at his face, he was smiling, and he had his hands resting on his gun belt. He was tall and broad across the shoulders. At first, I felt afraid, but then I started to feel a little embarrassed when I saw the marshal's star pinned to his shirt.

"I -I - I," I tried to apologize, but I was fumbling over my words.

He started to laugh and Clark ran to me and said, "This is Marshall Reeves. He was chasing those men we captured back at the Crossing. He left his deputies to take them into custody. He came here to bring us back. He says it's really dangerous up ahead, and he is going on to talk to the Indians and get this settled."

"He's right, Billy," said Reeves, "I am Deputy Marshal Bass Reeves, and I am very grateful what you and Clark did back there at the Crossing. Those were very dangerous men and you two took your lives in your hands to capture them." He reached out to take my hand and shake it.

"I'm pleased to meet you, Billy, but," he added in a much sterner voice, "I can't permit you to continue on. It's too dangerous out here. Captain Watson is just a few days ahead and we have some very unhappy Indians." He paused, looked at both of us and said, "So, you young bucks, you might as well turn your herd around now and head on back. You will never get this herd to market this year. As least, not until we have this Indian thing settled. I am going on ahead to see if I can defuse this standoff. We have the outlaws in a jail now. I just hope I can convince the Chief."

I guessed he was waiting for Clark and me to mount up, and like dogs with our tails between our legs, to head for home. I looked at Clark's face and I could see the determination in his eyes. I was sure he could see it in mine as well. The marshal had gotten on his horse and was ready to ride on, when he looked back at both of us. I think he sensed it, too, that we were not interested in turning back.

"Boys, I hope that look on your faces is not what I think it is," the marshal said as he glared at us.

Clark and I exchanged glances and I spoke up, "Marshal, I believe we can help."

Reeves let out a howl of a laugh and said, "Help? *Help?* Son, we are dealing with a volatile situation here, and I don't need a wet-behind-the-ears farmhand and a tenderfoot Easterner getting in my way. Now, git on home!" He turned north and began to trot off, then he stopped and turned around again. "Did you hear what I said? Now, Git!"

Clark and I still did not budge. For one thing, I was not a wet-behind-the-ears farmhand and although Clark was from the East, he was no longer a tenderfoot. We had been on the trail for over three weeks. We knew we could handle any situation.

This time Clark tried to explain to the marshal. "Sir, if you would just listen for a moment, I believe Billy is right. We can help. I understand that Billy's father is a friend of those Indians and maybe he can explain what happened and they just might believe him." Clark paused, not sure if he should say more or not.

Reeves just sat there on his horse with a blank stare on his face, looking at the two of us. He shook his head and said, "Do you expect me to believe that pile of—" he stopped short and then looked at me. "Who is his daddy that you think those Indians will believe him?"

Clark darted a look at me and I nodded to let him know it was all right to tell him.

Clark blurted out, "His father is Bill Pecos!"

Now Reeves was laughing harder than before, and in between chuckles, he said, "You expect *me* to believe *that!*"

"Yes, we do, sir," Clark offered respectfully. Clark then turned to me and said, "Show him the letter from your father."

I reached into my pants pocket, walked over to the marshal, and stretched up to hand him the letter. He grabbed it unbelievingly and began to read. You could see the look on his face change as he realized we were telling the truth. Reeves snorted through his nose and grinned sheepishly. He handed the letter back to me and said,

"Well, if that don't beat all I have ever seen! I know your daddy. Why, he helped me get this job. I remember him talking to Judge Isaac C. Parker - you know, the 'hanging judge'? He told him I would be perfect for this job." Then he looked down at me, "And you are his son? Why didn't you tell me before?" he paused. "I'm not sure how much help you'll be with the Indians, but, well, what the heck, come on, boys, let's get these longhorns moving and find the Captain."

With that, Reeves pulled his horse around and galloped to the front of the herd. Clark and I gave out a big yelp, jumped on our horses and started back on the trail. We gave each other a knowing grin and we continued to head north. We both had great confidence in ourselves. We each knew we had become better cowboys, better cowhands and the best of friends. It was good to have a friend.

CHAPTER 19

THE RIDE INTO
INDIAN COUNTRY

Reeves kept pretty much to himself. He came over to eat with us, but sat alone and didn't talk unless we asked a question. I broke the ice one evening as we sat around the fire.

"Are we getting close?" I asked.

Reeves did not look up from his plate of beans and biscuits. "Should be close enough before sundown tomorrow." I watched him as he ate. I knew he felt my eyes on him. Ever since that first time we met, he had not talked much at all. I had a hundred questions for him. *Where was he born? Had he ever been a slave? Does he have family? How did he get to be free? How long had he been a marshal?* And especially, *how did he meet my dad?* That morning I watched him shave. I wanted to know about him, but I was afraid he didn't want me to know anything about him. His clothes were always clean and neat. For a horseman, that's pretty good. He was always carrying his rifle laid across his saddle when he rode, and it seemed different than any rifle I had ever seen. I didn't feel comfortable getting too close to him, since I thought he liked being alone. After I asked the question about how close we were, I got the idea he didn't favor too much talking.

The next evening, he said we couldn't have a fire. So, we ate cold beans and sourdough biscuits. Just as we were about to finish supper and clean up, he spoke up.

"See those hills to the northwest of us?" He turned and pointed to some distant mountains over his shoulder. "Those are the Arbuckle Mountains, and Captain Watson is supposed to be held up there by a band of Cheyenne and Arapaho Indians. If I can get to the Chief, I hope to convince him we have those renegade outlaws in custody, and he will let the herd through."

"What is the Chief's name?" I asked.

Reeves glanced up at me as if he was trying to find a reason not to tell me that bit of information.

"Chief Little Raven," he replied grudgingly, but he sighed and continued, "He's a good man, but these hooligans keep trying to stir up trouble so they can sell guns to the Indians. The Chief is getting tired of all these shenanigans." He paused as he tossed his plate to me to wash up, "and I don't blame him. We are not doing the right thing with those Indians."

Chief Little Raven? The name sounded like someone my dad had talked about before. But then, my dad knew many Indians and he talked about a lot of them. Maybe my dad knew this one, too, I thought to myself.

When I looked back at Reeves, his face had become very sad as he looked off in the distance for what seemed a long time and then got up and headed for his bedroll.

That was the most he had talked on the whole trip so far. Clark and I washed up everything after supper, and the both of us fell asleep quickly as a thin slice of pink light faded behind the distant mountains. We knew tomorrow would be an eventful day.

CHAPTER 20

MEETING UP WITH THE INDIANS

"Let's go! We gotta get movin'." The loud voice of the marshal woke me up in the morning. I opened my eyes, and it was still dark. There was not even a hint of morning light etched in the eastern sky. I tried looking at my pocket watch, but it was too dark to tell the time.

"Why so early?" I questioned.

"We have to move fast today, and I want you boys with me. I'm not leaving you here to get in trouble, and I don't want anyone to know we have your herd out here. I'm going to have a big enough problem with the Captain's situation; I don't need another."

His voice seemed tense and serious. Clark and I looked at each other in the dark as we put on our boots and saddled the horses. We knew that today we wouldn't be asking a lot of questions.

Reeves did not waste time. He was mounted and off in a moment, and both Clark and I had to hurry to catch up with him. We did not start a fire, just like last night. There was no breakfast, not even coffee. I figured Reeves felt a fire just might alert the Indians.

As we rode, I was becoming very hungry, and I'm sure Clark was feeling the same. I took out my watch to check the time. It was now nine o'clock so I guessed we had been riding hard for about four hours. Then, for no apparent reason, Reeves slowed to a trot. He turned his head to one side and, out the corner of his mouth, said, "Stay close boys, we are being followed. Don't say a word; do you hear me? Let me do all the talking, if you want to get out of this alive."

Clark and I moved our horses closer to each other and moved closer to Reeves. At first, I did not believe him. I saw no one and did not hear a sound. The morning was so quiet and peaceful. Suddenly there were Indians all around – everywhere. They came out of nowhere and they had surprised me. There must have been twenty, maybe more.

I had not noticed before, but Reeves had tied a white handkerchief around the barrel of his rifle, and now he was slowly lifting it up above our heads. We continued our trot forward, but now several Indians had pulled in front of us, and Reeves guided his horse to follow them. Of course, we stayed right with him.

I was thinking to myself how in just a few days I had met a black man, and now I was surrounded by Indians. I did not have much experience with either. I had heard stories about Indians from my dad and others, but I had never been this close to them. Their skin was dark, but not like Reeves'. I had heard them called 'redskins' but their skin did not seem red. It was more like a brown that seemed to glow in the sun, almost like copper. Most of them were completely bare-chested and they did not wear long pants like we did. They had skins wrapped around their waists, tied with strips of leather. Some had feathers hanging from around their heads. I knew from my dad's stories about his Indian friends that the feathers were like badges of honor. The older-looking Indians had more; the younger ones had less or none. I tried not to stare at them, but I could tell many of them who were riding beside us did not seem much older than me, and the oldest seemed to be Clark's age. I wondered if he had noticed this, too.

We rode in silence for what seemed hours, however I kept looking at my watch and it had not been even an hour since we first saw the Indians. I did not see another herd or Captain Watson. I didn't want to look around too much either. I felt many pairs of eyes on me and I was afraid to look at them eye to eye. I wanted to make eye contact with Clark to see how he was doing, but my fear won out. I kept my head down and tried to stare straight ahead and, soon, I could see a village ahead of us.

As we entered the village, there were many more Indians - young boys and girls, mothers holding babies, and older men and women. It was if I were riding into my own town and seeing the same people, only their skin was a different color and the clothes they wore were not the same. Now, many more pairs of eyes watched us. *What were they thinking? What did they think about my skin color? What did they think about my clothes? Were they afraid of me? Did they hate me? Are our differences greater than our similarities?* Suddenly, the horses stopped, and I was jolted out of my thinking stupor.

I had to stretch up in my saddle to see what was happening. As I looked over Reeves' shoulder, I saw someone who was probably the Chief. He was very regal looking. Many feathers adorned his head, and his face was old but kind, like a grandfather. I guessed he was a grandfather. I was sure many of the young Indian braves and the younger children I saw around me were his. I wondered how they felt to have such an important man as Chief Little

Raven as their father or grandfather. I wondered if he was always traveling away from the tribe and his family, or if they had a lot of time to spend with him.

Finally, Reeves got down off his horse, and I could see what was happening much better. They began to talk, but I couldn't hear them. The Chief seemed angry, and he shook his head 'no' several times. Reeves continued to talk, and it seemed he was almost pleading with the Chief. Finally, I saw Reeves drop his shoulders and head and slowly turn around and head for his horse. He mounted and turned his horse to leave the camp. As he passed us, we turned and began to follow.

Suddenly, the Chief called out loudly, "Wait!" Reeves stopped and turned back around. I too, turned around, and I saw that the Chief was looking straight at me. He walked toward me and continued. "I must speak with boy!"

I felt my heart start to pound in my chest and I spun around to look at Reeves.

He leaned back in his saddle and said, "The boy is with me. He has nothing to do with our disagreement."

But the Chief was serious, and he again said, "I must speak with boy!"

Reeves started to argue with the Chief, but held back. The marshal looked at me, and I saw confusion and bewilderment on his face for the first time. I was not sure what to do. I stared at Reeves for an answer, and he nodded to me to go with the Chief.

I dismounted and handed my reins to Clark, who had a look of complete fear on his face. Now I was afraid too, but I cautiously and slowly walked towards the Chief. As I looked at his face, I saw a smile almost creep across his lips. When I was close enough to touch him, he turned to the side, which startled me, but he motioned with his hand to enter his teepee. I hesitated for a moment, glancing back at Clark and Reeves. I then turned, stooped down and entered inside.

Once inside, I stood up and look around. There were drawings all over the inner walls and many blankets on the floor. There was a small fire in the middle. The Chief walked completely around me and then went to the far side to sit. He beckoned me to sit next to him. I felt uncomfortable as he continued to watch me. Very slowly, he began to grin and soon his lips parted to show his teeth in a broad smile. This happy expression on his face soon helped me to feel more at ease, although I was not sure why I was here. Finally, the Chief began to speak.

"I know who you are. You are son of Bill Pecos. Are you not?"

I was stunned that he knew who I was. I stuttered out a reply, "Y-yes, I-I am." Now he started to laugh out loud, and I still didn't know what to make of this happening. I wanted to ask how he knew, but no words would come out. The Chief could sense my puzzlement and then he started to explain.

"I knew who you were when I saw blanket strapped to your saddle. There is only one blanket like that. I gave to your father many years ago when we were both much younger. He told me when he had son, he would give it to him as token of our continuing friendship for many generations to come. Your father is good man. I trust him. And, as his son, I trust you. If you tell me that the men who tried to destroy my village and stole my horses are captured, and that they will pay for crimes, I will believe you."

"Yes, they are captured. I-I helped capture them myself," I blurted out. I felt a little embarrassed to say that to the Chief. I watched as his eyes got wide and started to twinkle and a grin again came across his face.

"Please, you must tell me story," he insisted, "Your father told me many stories when we were together. We would laugh for hours."

I did tell him the story and we laughed too.

After what probably seemed like a long time, we emerged from the teepee. Reeves and Clark had a look of shock on their faces as they saw us standing there - Chief Little Raven with his arm around me; and we were both laughing out loud. He turned to an Indian who seemed to be standing guard at his door and told him something in their own language. I did not know what he said, but the Indian ran and jumped on a horse and sped out of the village. The Chief raised his arms and spoke in a loud voice to all his people who had gathered around. It was as if he was shouting good news to them. As he finished, they began to talk excitedly to themselves. He again put his arm around me and escorted me to Reeves.

Reeves got off his horse as Chief Little Raven approached, and the chief spoke, "I have sent word to let the Watson herd through. You may go in peace."

Reeves' mouth dropped open, but no words came out. I mounted my horse, and as I turned to face the Chief, he reached up to shake my hand. As our eyes met, we realized we had made a bond of trust. No more words were needed, for us or for anyone else. Reeves was still in disbelief about what had happened. I began to ride out of the village, but this time, I could look the people in the eyes. They were smiling and waving to me. It was now Reeves who was following *me*, and there was no Indian escort.

I was again beginning to feel very proud about myself and about my dad. For this moment, I felt much taller in the saddle as we headed back to my herd. I knew we had a lot to do to catch up to Captain Watson, but I knew everything would turn out fine.

I noticed Reeves. He was still dumbfounded. He wanted to talk, but I offered no comment. He was in the awkward position of having to ask all the questions now. Finally, he could not contain it anymore and he spoke.

"Just what happened back there? The Chief told me in no uncertain terms, that he would *not* let that cattle drive through without my turning those outlaws over to him, and I told him I just couldn't do that. But," he gathered his thoughts and continued, "he sees you, you go in the tent with him and you come out bosom buddies. . . ." His voice trailed off as if he was trying to figure it out himself.

I looked over to Clark, and I could tell he knew what happened. He did not need me to explain what just went on between me and Chief Little Raven.

CHAPTER 21

WE FINALLY FOUND
CAPTAIN WATSON

We had been pushing the longhorns, and ourselves, real hard - long days, short nights and eating in the saddle. It took us a couple of days, but we finally caught up with Captain Watson and his herd. We planned to keep the two herds separate until the Captain could look over my herd. Late in the evening, we finally met for supper. As we entered the campsite, a tall, thin man with a mustache and a long, thin beard approached. He was nicely dressed in a uniform I was not familiar with. He had long flowing, dark hair coming out the back of his hat.

"Thank God, we are all safe! You did a great job, Reeves, convincing that chief. My hat is off to you! You saved all our lives! I thought we would all be dead soon."

By now all the men in the camp were gathering around us. There must have been a half dozen. They were talking among themselves and nodding and voicing agreement with the bearded man, whom I soon realized must have been Captain John J. Watson.

As the marshal dismounted, he seemed a little embarrassed. He sheepishly looked up to me and then back to the crowd who was now huddled close enough to Reeves that they were shaking his hand and patting him on the back.

Captain Watson broke through the crowd and started to shake Reeves hand. "You are a hero, Reeves. I believe..."

Just at that moment, Reeves cut him off and confessed, "Don't thank me, Captain, I didn't have that much to do with it." The Captain and the men froze for a moment and then began to look at each other. "No, sir," the marshal continued, "The man you need to thank is young Billy here. The Chief took a liking to him and that is the reason your herd was allowed to continue through."

"So, you are the young Billy Pecos," The Captain said as he moved next to my horse. "I should have known. Your father and I have trailed many cattle drives together, and I can say that, on more than one occasion, your father saved my life. Much of what I know today, I learned from your father. Bill is a wonderful man. Young Billy's just like his father, isn't he men?" he said to his riders, and I heard the men talking in agreement. Looking back up at me, he said, "Come on down from your horse, young man. We have a lot to talk about."

As I landed on the ground, I was immediately surrounded by men who all patted me on the back, talked loudly to me, thanked me, and swiftly ushered me along with the crowd to the fire. I was quickly seated on a bench near the fire. At this point, I was speechless. A hundred feelings were rushing through my body. My head began to feel light and people were moving so quickly around me, and so much talking was going on that I felt as if my head was swimming in a whirlpool. So many thoughts were going through my head that I couldn't seem to latch on to even one of them. I couldn't seem to even put together one word of my own, let alone one sentence. My heart was pounding like a drum in my chest, and my eyes were trying to focus on one thing, but they couldn't. The fire before me seemed to be growing wider and taller, and the noise was louder and more confusing . . .

"I think it was just too much excitement."

"No, it was my fault. I didn't let them eat properly the last couple of days. He just needs a good meal."

"Let him have some air."

"He'll be fine when he wakes up."

I heard the voices, but I could not see the faces, just darkness. I realized my eyes were closed, and I tried to open them, but the light was blinding. I squeezed them shut again. I didn't know who was talking, but it sounded like several different men.

"He's just a young fella'. Drivin' all those longhorns can wear you out!"

"I think he's comin' around. Bring me a cup of that coffee—from the really strong pot!"

I felt hands and arms lifting me up, and they put me back on the bench. A cup touched my lips, and I tried to sip, but it was too hot, and I pulled back.

"What are you tryin' to do, Jake? Burn his mouth?"

"I ain't gonna' burn his mouth. It just startled him."

"Here, give him a drink of water first."

I felt the cool water splash on my dry lips. I was trying to lick my lips when the mouth of a canteen was pushed between them. I took several gulps and closed my mouth. Now that I was sitting up, the brightness of the sun was not directly in my face, and I could open my eyes.

"Well, Mr. Billy, I see you are back with the living." I heard someone speak to me, and then I heard him yell, "He's gonna be fine Captain!"

"Good! Put him in the wagon and let's ride." It was Watson speaking. "Once we had word the Indians would let us through, I sent the herd on ahead with my cowhands. We have a lot of trail to make up, and a lot of time. We'll catch up with the herd and Jake, you do the same."

I could see several men riding off as I barely opened my eyes. I felt someone lift me to my feet, and my body slowly began to come alive. I tried to get myself up on the wagon but I needed some help to do it.

As I started to become more coherent, I remembered last night. At least, I thought it was last night. *What happened to me? Why did I feel so weak?* As I began to sort things out, someone started to talk to me.

"Good morning, Mr. Billy. Too much excitement last night, huh? You slept here, by the wagon, so's I could look in on ya."

I tried to open my mouth but nothing came out.

"Just take it easy. Everything will be fine. And don't worry about your spread. The boys are going to take real good care of your longhorns and I'm gonna take real good care of you. I'm Jake, and I'm the cook for this outfit. But more'n not you'll hear the boys call me the 'hash slinger', the 'biscuit shooter' or 'Cooky.' But my name is Jake." He whistled at the horses and soon we were moving. "Got to catch up with the herd," he said.

Jake had a face full of whiskers. Whereas the Captain had a neatly trimmed beard, Jake's scraggy beard almost covered his wrinkled, weather-beaten face. His clothes seemed too big for him, and you would think he would be fat, since he was always around food every day, but he was as skinny a man as I had ever seen. When he talked, you noticed he did not have many teeth, and the ones he had were brown and crooked. His hat was turned up in the front and made his face appear more comical than it already was.

Jake continued, "Mighty fine thing you did back there, young fella'. All these cowhands are sorely grateful. Yes, sir, you are a hero." He whistled again and began to work the mule team hard to catch up with cattle drive.

Oh, yes, I was starting to remember now. My head was beginning to clear. The meeting with Chief Little Raven, catching up with Captain Watson. Oh, yes, Captain Watson. I remembered his face and how dapper he looked in his neat uniform. I remembered the hoard of men around me and all the noise and the fire and . . . that was the last I remembered. Jake noticed I was struggling with the recollection of what happened and he began to talk to me.

"You were probably just plum worn out young Billy. Startin' off on a cattle drive by yersef' back in West Texas. Capturin' those outlaws at the crossin', meetin' up with Injuns; not to mention foilin' the robbery back in your town before all that. There's just so much a body can take." He stopped reciting my tale to steer the chuck wagon through a rocky patch.

How did he know so much about me? Who told him all those tales? I guessed it was Clark. Clark. I had not seen him in a long time it seemed. I hoped he was all right. I finally mustered up enough energy to ask about Clark.

"Where is my friend Clark? Is he all right?" I muttered as my mouth was dry again, and I began to look for that canteen.

"That's a fine young man, too. Why, he stayed with you all night, barely sleepin' hisself. Got a funny way of talkin' at times, but good folk." He paused as if he had answered my question.

"But where is he now?" I asked.

"Oh, he's with Captain Watson. They took a fancy to each other. I think that young man has decided to stay on and ride all the way to Abilene, and the Captain is gonna be teachin' him the ropes of headin' up a cattle drive, sorta speak. Seems they both hail from the same big city back East. That young man spoke very highly of you, young Billy. Said you saved his life. He was sayin' how that experience changed him forever. Said he tried to talk his daddy into lettin' him ride with you, but his daddy told him 'No'. So, that Clark, why, he lit out anyway. Said after he almost lost his life, he wanted to get out of the bankin' business and become a cowboy. And he will, ifin' he hangs out with this bunch, as sure as shootin'."

Well, what do you know! Clark lied about his dad letting him go with me! That little rascal! That was why he was not going back home; his dad would blister his hide. Well, maybe not blister his hide, since he was a little older, but his dad would probably be really mad. As I thought about Clark not going home with me, I got a little sad. We had become good friends. Even though he was older than me, he never treated me as a child. He trusted me, and he was willing to learn from me. I was sad he was not returning with me, but I was glad he had found his future. Clark the cowboy. Hmm.... Had a nice ring to it.

As I continued to think about all that had happened over the last several weeks, I was starting to enjoy the ride with Jake. Without realizing it, I was beginning to relax and feel comfortable out here. I could imagine my dad in this same place. I could see the Arbuckle Mountains all around us and the beautiful valleys that flowed between their ridges. I imagined that maybe he was as content as I was right now. The sky was so blue. I had never noticed how blue it was. A few wisps of clouds gathered here and there across its reaches—dancing ever-changing designs in the sky.

I had become lost in all my thoughts and had not noticed the day was passing quickly. Not only had we had caught up with the herd, we had passed them. I began looking for my cattle, and I noticed that they were now mixed in with the other longhorns. As I was looking over the herd, I saw the Captain gallop up to the wagon.

"You look fit as a fiddle, young Billy," he said, "I guess you are ready to head for home now."

Just then, Clark rode up at a fast pace and pulled up at the last minute next to the wagon. "How is that for riding, Billy? Pretty good, huh?"

"Real good, Clark. You are becoming a great cowboy," I responded. Then I asked, "Where are our longhorns?"

Clark started to answer, but the Captain interrupted him. "I bought them, Billy. The nicest, fattest, healthiest longhorns I have ever seen. Since I will be getting top dollar for them in Abilene, I am willing to pay you top dollar, too, especially since you saved our lives back there. Of course, minus the five dollars I left for you at the crossing with Mr. Chisholm. Billy, we counted one hundred forty-five. That was a lot for just two cowhands. How many did you lose on the trail?"

At the same time, Clark and I both answered back, "Only two!"

"Well, that *is* mighty impressive," the Captain said. "You two *are* pretty good cowboys!" He continued, "Now, at seven dollars a head, that's . . ."

"Uh, Captain," I interrupted. I cleared my throat, and after glancing at Clark, I straightened up and said, "You *did* say they were the finest you had ever seen. And since I was planning on taking them to market myself . . . Well, I don't think seven dollars a head is enough. You'll be sure to get ten, maybe twelve dollars a head, and I am sure not a penny less."

The captain looked me square in the eyes, and I could tell he was pondering my offer. Just when I thought he was not going to accept, he gave out this deep, laugh and broke into a big smile.

"You're a hard businessman, young Billy. And you are right. I'll get at least ten dollars for each of them. I owe you that much. So, I'll give you nine apiece," he paused to figure out the price, "that means I owe you . . . "

"One thousand three hundred, five dollars, sir," shot back Clark, "and if you take out the five dollars, it leaves one thousand, three hundred dollars even."

"Humm, good with numbers, too," he said to Clark, "I think you will come in real handy working for me." Then he scribbled on a piece of paper, turned to me and said, "Well, young Billy, take this and hand it to Jake. He will pay you."

He held out a note for me that he had written on a piece of paper.

"And when you are feeling spry enough to travel, you can take off. It's been a real pleasure doing business with you. Your dad would be proud." He started off but turned back quickly. "Oh, by the way, Marshal Reeves had to get back to the Crossing. He left early this morning. He said to tell you goodbye."

He paused, chuckled to himself and added, "He was still mighty mystified about how you saved the day. He figured it had to do something with your dad. So do I, but I'm not looking a gift horse in the mouth. Good luck, son. Give my regards to your dad for me. Tell him he has a son as grand as he is."

With that, the Captain was off to his herd. By now, Jake had stopped the wagon far enough in front of the herd that he could now begin cooking the evening meal. He was busy getting the fire going and setting out the big pots in which he had put water and an armful of potatoes. As I sat and watched Jake, Clark rode up again. He jumped off his horse and ran over to me.

"I've got good news, Billy," he said as he came closer to lean over to me and whispered, "There's something I have been wanting to tell you. But, well," as he started to stammer, "Well, Billy, as you might know already, I- I - I'm heading out to be a cowboy, and I am not going back with you."

"Never?" I asked.

"Well, not soon, anyway."

"Like you told me once before on the trail, 'A man's gotta do what a man's gotta do,' right?"

He forced a weak smile across his lips, but then, with a very guilty look on his face, he began to confess to me, "Billy, I lied about my dad letting me trail with you. He was afraid I couldn't do it, that I would fail. Billy you are only thirteen, and I am almost twenty-one, and I thought if you can do it, I can do it." He paused again and swallowed hard, "I ran away from home without my father's blessing."

He seemed relieved to finally tell me the truth.

"Billy," he continued, "when you get back, tell my dad and all my family, I'm alright, and that everything . . ." he sighed, "and I'll be fine and I'll come home one day, if they'll have me back."

I could detect a small tear in Clark's eye. I put my hand on his shoulder, and I told him, "You have done great. I could not have gotten this far without you. You were very brave back at town, and you saved my life after the storm and don't forget the Crossing, either. You are a hero. You can make sure I will tell your dad that, too. He will be as proud of you as I am, and somehow . . ."

I commenced to get a little choked, but started again. "You know, I never had an older brother, but if I did, I would want him to be just like you."

"Thanks, Billy," whispered Clark. Then after a long moment of stillness in which neither of us knew what else to say, Clark offered his hand and we shook then he broke the silence. "Good luck to you and be safe. I will see you one day, for sure." He mounted his horse and galloped off as fast as he could.

He couldn't hear me, but I added, "God's speed, Clark."

As I turned to Jake, he handed me an envelope, and said, "One thousand, three hundred dollars, on the button."

"Thanks, Jake. For this, and for taking care of me," I said as I took the envelope with one hand and shook his hand with the other. Darlin' and Princess were tied up to the back of the wagon, and I noticed that Darlin' was saddled and Princess had been packed with food and supplies. Jake looked up and saw me staring at the two horses.

"Well," he said, "I couldn't let you out on the trail without proper nourishment, now could I?"

"You are a good man, Jake. I'm going to miss you," I said, as I got on Darlin' and grabbed the reins for Princess. "Take care of Clark for me, will you? He has a great heart, and I don't want anything to happen to him."

"You betcha," answered Jake as he stood there next to his chuck wagon.

We waved good-bye to each other. I turned the horses south, and I set out for home. It was a very strange feeling now. I believed I felt lonelier now than when I started out weeks ago. At least then, I had my longhorns. Now, the cattle were gone, Clark was gone, and so were Marshal Reeves and Captain Watson and his cowhands and especially Jake. I bowed my head and said a prayer.

"Dear Lord, thank You for all the new friends I've met. Thank You for watching over me this far. Thanks for watching over my family and my dad. And I know You will continue to watch over me on my way home. Amen."

I knew God would help me during a very lonely ride home indeed.

CHAPTER

22

A New Friend on the Trail

The sun had barely crept over the ridge in the east when I awakened. In the dim light of morning, I dressed and decided on a good breakfast. The embers of the fire from the night before were still glowing. I added a few twigs and in a breath or two, the flames began to grow, and with a few more branches and limbs I found lying on the ground, the fire was big enough to cook on.

As I dug deeper in the grub bag Jake had made for me, I found some pickled eggs and a small slab of salt bacon, and some more of his biscuits. I tossed the bacon into the skillet and started the coffee. The smell was strong and full. I breathed in deeply through my nose and filled my lungs with the aroma. As much as I enjoyed cooking in the outdoors, I still liked my mom's cooking the best. I thought about her chicken and dumplings, cornbread, and the wild berry jams she made. I missed all those, and it made me more eager to get home. I was starting to feel the warm sun, which was now slowly edging upward, on my back. Its brightness was sending streaks of shadows and light far across the valley in front of me. As I look across the horizon before me, I was startled by the sight of a lone figure on a horse. He was standing very still in the distance. I reached for my rifle, but I didn't take it out. I couldn't make out who it was because it was so far away. I continued to eat breakfast, and then, after putting out the fire and cleaning up, I broke camp. I got on my horse, and I noticed the figure was still in the same spot. I tried not to let on I was watching, but I also tried not to let the horseman out of my sight.

I came to a small stream and I stopped, dismounted, and let the horses water. As I leaned against my saddle, I looked back to the distant hill, and the figure was gone. I quickly glanced around, but I didn't see it again. I imagined he was gone, and I didn't worry about it anymore.

I was not pushing the horses hard, but we were moving at a nice pace, trotting back towards the Crossing much faster than we came the first time. The sun was now high in the Oklahoma sky, but I did not want to stop again. The horses were watered and they had eaten when we stopped earlier.

I was lost in thought about getting home and seeing my family and especially Samantha. I wondered if she would be sad her brother was not coming home. I wondered if she would be glad to see me. As my mind wandered into many thoughts of home, I was startled again by the same figure, only this time he was in front of me to the right on a high ridge. Again, he was very still, and I tried not to let on that I had seen him. *Who was he? Why was he following me? Was he following me? What did he want? Where was he going?* I continued to ride, and he stayed in the same place. I was soon directly across from him and as I passed, I figured he'd be about thousand yards away - clearly out of gunshot range for him or me. By now I was sure he knew that I knew he was there. He had not tried to hide himself at all. As I continued to ride past him he was now behind me, and still, he had not moved. It was not the marshal. This figure was much too small for him. I did not think it was a cowboy because I saw no hat. It couldn't be Mr. Chisholm, because Mr. Chisholm was much too heavy. *Was it an Indian?* I saw no feathers. *Who could it be, and why?* The thought of someone, cowboy or Indian, following me made me a little nervous. Just like before, when I would briefly turn away, the figure would disappear. I was beginning to think it was a ghost. Again, I searched around for him but to no avail. However, I felt sure I would see him again. I eventually stopped to bed down for the night, knowing there was someone out there watching me.

The next morning as I awakened, I began to look for my visitor, and, sure enough, he was there again, still about a thousand yards away. I still didn't know who he was, but now I felt that he was not here to harm me. It was as if he was waiting for me or wanting to meet me. During breakfast, I didn't notice him anymore. I settled down to some more salt bacon, pickled eggs, biscuits and coffee. I sat, leaning against Darlin's saddle, which I had propped up against a large boulder.

I was casually eating my breakfast and drinking my coffee when I got the scare of my life. I looked up to see an Indian standing right before me. It scared me so much that I jumped to my feet - biscuit, bacon, and egg going three different directions and the cup of coffee splashing down the front of me. The hot coffee burned through my pants legs, and I began jumping up and down to cool down my legs.

As I looked up at the Indian before me, I saw him laughing uncontrollably. In an instant, I stopped being scared and started being mad, and, without any hesitation, I charged him and tackled him to the ground. My arms were wrapped tightly around his body as we rolled across the dirt. I thought I was in control, but he quickly gained the edge and turned his body in such a way that he flipped me off, and I landed about ten feet from him. As I jumped up and turned around, I looked for something I could use as a weapon. My rifle was still slid underneath my saddle where I had left it while sleeping. I tried looking for a rock, but I couldn't find one to throw. I glanced down and saw one of the eggs lying on the ground beside me, so I picked it up and whizzed it at his head. When he saw it coming, he ducked and the egg smacked his horse right between the eyes, and in a flash, it reared up and ran out of sight. I saw the look on that Indian's face as he watched his horse run off. I could not keep myself from laughing. He turned around to charge me but stopped in his tracks. He, too, began to laugh again and pointed a finger at my head. I reached up to where he was pointing, and I felt a hunk of biscuit smashed to the side of my face. As I pulled it off, he laughed even harder. The comedy of it made me laugh, too. Here we were, both laughing at each other and at ourselves so hard, we soon collapsed on the ground, continuing to laugh. In a moment, we finally regained our composure and we both took deep sighs to get our breath back.

I looked at him. He was about my age. There were no feathers in the beaded cloth that held his hair back. He was wearing breeches made of animal skins, and he wore moccasins, too. He had bands tied tightly around his upper arms, and a bow and quiver was strapped to his back. His face was smooth and brown. His eyes were so dark, they must have been black. At once, I began to feel at ease. His face appeared kind, and I didn't think he wanted to harm me. As we sat there, I started to talk to him.

"Why have you been following me? What do you want with me? Who are you?" As I talked I could see the puzzled look on his face, and I realized he did not understand anything I was saying.

"Do you understand English?" I asked. Still, he had that look of bewilderment on his face. I realized talking to him would get us nowhere. As he watched me struggle with what to say to him, he interrupted me and pointed his finger at my chest, touching me lightly. "Bil-ly," he said.

"Yes!" I answered excitedly, "I'm Billy, and," but before I could ask him his name, he pointed to himself and said, "Okomi".

"O-ko-mi," I repeated very slowly as I pointed to him, "Bil-ly," I said as I pointed to myself.

Okomi nodded his head in great excitement, and we both seemed relieved that we were finally communicating. I did not get to finish my breakfast, as it was now all over the ground. I bent over to pick up the cup and plate. When I looked up, I saw Okomi take off running after his horse. He was gone for almost a half an hour, but then returned, pulling his horse behind him. I had been packing, and I was soon ready to hit the trail again. As I mounted Darlin', Okomi mounted his horse and appeared to be waiting for me. I dug my heels into Darlin' and she responded by leaping into a gallop. Okomi also nudged his horse with his heels, and he let out a wail as he, too, burst into a gallop and was soon alongside me. He glanced at me with a smile and dug even deeper into the sides of his horse, and took off ahead of me. I got the feeling he wanted to race.

I dropped the reins to Princess. I leaned forward and squeezed my heels into Darlin's sides. She knew what to do, and she exploded into a dead run. It was just a matter of moments, and we were again side-by-side. Okomi and his horse did not even appear to be working hard. He seemed to only be humoring me by letting me run alongside of him. With another wail, his horse soared out ahead of us and was flying like the wind. In a blink of an eye, he was so far ahead of me, I knew I could never catch him. I eased up on Darlin' and headed back to get Princess. Okomi slowed down and turned around to come back to us. I conceded defeat, and Okomi knew he had won. He was grinning ear to ear. The Indian beat a white man. I was sure he would be telling this story to all his friends back home. We rode for a long time without talking. I could feel he wanted to talk, just like I did, but neither one of us knew the other's language.

I could tell that he was from the Arapaho tribe - the same tribe that Chief Little Raven led. Back at the village I remembered seeing the men wearing breechcloths made of deerskins. The men I saw on horseback had leather moccasins and leggings. They had beautiful beads sewn into their clothing. Their armbands and headbands had beads sewn into them as well. Okomi was dressed in the same kinds of garments as I saw in the village. He had to be Arapaho. I noticed, however, that he did not have a feather in his hair like many others did back in the village. I didn't know much about this Arapaho brave, but I wanted to find a way to communicate with him.

As we came upon a small riverbed that was almost dry, Okomi jumped quickly off his horse and led him to water. He did not have a saddle - only a couple of blankets he rode on. He did not have a bridle for his horse - only a braided rope tied around the horse's muzzle. I was going to offer my canteen to him, but I watched as he and his horse drank from the water at the same time, right next to each other. Darlin' and Princess both walked up next to Okomi's horse and were drinking from a shallow pool. I decided to join them. I lay on my stomach, on the other side of Okomi, and drank directly out of the river.

It was soon late afternoon, and I was sure Okomi intended to travel with me for a while longer. He did not show any inclination to leave. We were now riding our horses at a very leisurely pace, and he turned to me as if to speak. Instead of words coming out of his mouth, he rubbed his stomach and brought his fingers, held close together, to his mouth. He had a questioning look on his face. I assumed he was trying to tell me he was hungry or he wanted to eat. Then he pointed to my stomach and rubbed his own again. I decided to copy him and see what would happen. I rubbed my stomach and then brought my clenched fingers to my mouth. Instantly, he pointed to himself then he motioned off into the distance with one hand, and with his other hand, he took off his bow and grabbed an arrow.

In a second, he was off his horse and scurrying very quickly through the sage. Before I knew it, he had disappeared into the brush. I dismounted and tied all three horses up to a nearby scrub tree. After searching the ground for sticks and twigs and gathering them to start a fire, I heard a rustling from the direction of where Okomi had gone. As quickly as he had disappeared, he reappeared - only this time, he had a dead rabbit in his hand. He had shot it right through the neck with an arrow.

Supper that night was especially good. Okomi had skinned the rabbit and kept its fur. He had gutted it and placed a long sapling through it and held it over the fire. As he was holding it in his hands, I fashioned two limbs in the shape of a "Y" and shoved them deep into the soil on either side of the fire. I took the rabbit out of Okomi's hand and placed the sapling he was holding between the limbs. He moved back as I took over the cooking. He acknowledged my handiwork with a nod of his head. Finally, one point for the white man. He won the race. He got the rabbit, but I will get it cooked. Tomorrow, I told myself, I would get the meal.

23
CHAPTER

FINALLY BACK IN TEXAS

We had stopped at the Red River Station for a short time to buy some supplies, and I needed to pay Mr. Chisholm for the clothes I bought from him. I tried to give him twenty dollars, but he would only accept half of that. He was satisfied, and we shook on our deal. I tried to get Okomi to try on some cowboy pants, but he refused. He even refused a hat when Mr. Chisholm offered it. But, when it came to the hard rock candy and the taffy, he could not refuse. After Mr. Chisholm let him try a piece of each, he was hooked. He even offered Mr. Chisholm one of his blankets for more of the candy. Mr. Chisholm refused to trade but did wrap up a small bag of the candy and gave it to Okomi. I tried to explain that Mr. Chisholm and I were good friends, and now he and Mr. Chisholm were friends. I was not sure he understood, but he was happy to get the candy anyway. We were almost ready to bid farewell to the crossing, when Mr. Chisholm stopped us and gave me a letter from Marshal Reeves. My hands were full, so I stuffed it in my back pocket. I thought I would read it later.

Okomi and I had become good friends. The language problem was still there, but we had learned to communicate in signs and gestures. He had been teaching me to shoot his bow and arrows, and I had been teaching him to shoot with the gun. I could never get the arrow to go straight, and he hated the noise the gun made, but we had fun trying. We shared horses. Riding bare back with no stirrups was hard for me, and on my horse, Okomi never used them. Plus, he complained the saddle was too hard. Except for those differences, we had many things in common. Although we used different ways, we both enjoyed hunting. We both loved horses and we both loved to eat.

I remembered one night as we sat around the campfire, and we were both tired from a long day, I began wondering what his name meant in his language. I had always heard that Indian names were important and had great meaning to the person and to the tribe. I looked at Okomi and I repeated his name over several times.

"Okomi, Okomi, O-ko-mi,"

At first, he appeared puzzled, but I repeated it several times again, but, then, it seemed as if he suddenly understood. He got excited as he jumped up from where he sat around the fire. He then got on all fours. He looked at the moon and began to howl. He was very comical as he scampered around the fire, crawling on his knees and using his hands as if he were trying to paw the sky.

I understood! "Coyote!" I screeched. "It means coyote!" He was still racing around the campfire, howling to the top of his lungs. I decided to join him. There we were - jumping around, pawing the air, and howling at the moon as loud as we could, laughing until our sides hurt!

Although I missed my family back home, and I was eager to get there, I knew that one day soon Okomi would be leaving me. It seemed he realized I would be home any day now, and we would have to part as he would head back to his home.

It was nice to finally see familiar territory. The closer I got to home, the quieter I got and the more homesick I became. I thought Okomi noticed that I was not communicating as much as before, and I believed he understood my feelings. I was probably looking a little sad, too, and he would try to cheer me up with funny antics. He would ride backwards on his horse and make funny faces at me, or, whenever we would stop to water the horses or to stretch our legs, he would act silly by dancing around in circles or by running back and forth like a crazy animal. He could always make me laugh, and he knew it. I was so glad to have him ride back with me.

We were now only hours away from home. I had almost forgotten about *him*, until I looked up on the crest of the hill before us. There he was! It was almost as if he was waiting for me to return. I stopped Darlin' in her tracks as I stared straight ahead. Okomi stopped too, looked at me, and then followed my eyes to where I was watching. There he was, the stallion, standing in an open area with a ridge of mountains behind him and a narrow gorge between two steep ridges. I did not make a move or a sound. I figured if I made one move toward him or made even the slightest of sounds, he would bolt through the gorge, and he would be gone. Okomi pointed to the horse we were watching on the hill and then pointed to me.

"No, he is not mine yet. But one day . . ." I did not finish the sentence, because I did not know how I would capture him. I started to turn Darlin' to continue to head for home, but Okomi grabbed my arm as he leaned across his horse. I stopped and looked at him, wondering what he wanted. He had a strange, wild look in his eyes. He slowly pointed to me, then himself, and then he reached his hand out toward the horse on the hill, and, as he extended his hand, fingers wide, he clutched his hand as if grabbing something. Then he brought his clutched fist to me and offered it, opening his hand to me.

"You will help me capture him?" I questioned, knowing he did not understand anything I was saying. He repeated the motion again, and we both knew what to do. I nodded my approval, and with a shake of his head, he turned to the stallion and began to slowly trot toward him. I followed closely behind, believing he had a plan in mind. As we got closer, the great horse became skittish and was jumping left and right. Okomi stopped and motioned for me to circle around the hill that was behind the white horse. I walked Darlin' around him, never getting any closer and not moving too fast. He was watching us as we split - not sure if he should run between us, around us or away from us. Soon, I was behind him and I climbed the ridge. Standing on the top, I could see him. He was pawing the ground and swaying back and forth. I could also see Okomi as he slowly moved toward the stallion. I crept closer to the edge of the ridge. It was a straight drop off to the bottom of the gorge, maybe ten or more feet down. The other ridge was only a few feet away, which made the passage very narrow. This would be perfect. If Okomi could get the stallion to run through the gorge, I believed I could jump on him, and then he would be mine.

I had taken my lariat and the rope was opened just enough to pass over his head. I took the other end of it and tied it around my waist. I moved closer to the edge. I could see Okomi watching me, and, once he saw me in place, he raced towards the great horse. In a flash, the stallion turned and started up the narrow canyon just like I hoped he would do. I quickly tried to move into place, but the soft rocks under my feet gave way, and I began to slip.

Then, an enormous rock started to break away from the ridge beneath my feet. I struggled to keep my balance, but I couldn't. As the white stallion passed under me, I could only try to leap back to the top of the mountain, but, instead, I lost my footing and began to fall to the ravine floor beneath me. In that brief second, I felt as if I would die on the rocks below. As I watched myself plunge to my death, I was suddenly jerked to a stop only a few inches from the bottom. I was now dangling, tied to my rope, which was caught around another rock jutting out above me. I felt as if my heart had stopped beating. My body was now swaying from the rock on a loop I had intended for the stallion.

I could hear Okomi calling to me, "Bil-l-l-ly!" "Bil-l-l-ly!" he repeated over and over. I was so out of breath, I couldn't respond. The rope was wrapped around my waist, and it made it hard to breathe, let alone speak out. I could hear his calls getting closer and closer, and soon he was standing above me from where I was hanging. He was so surprised to look down and see me hanging there below him. He tossed me another rope, and I tied that one to my waist too. I felt myself being hoisted up the side of the canyon. As I reached the top, I saw that he tied the other end to Darlin' and used her to pull me to safety. I was breathing heavily, and I still could not speak. Okomi was checking my body for any serious injuries, but found none. Except for the scare of a lifetime, I believed I was fine. As we looked at each other, we commenced to chuckle, and then we both started to laugh out loud. For a situation that almost killed me just minutes before, it all seemed so comical now. I finally caught my breath, and I looked down at the rocks below. The narrow gorge was now filled with boulders, blocking any entrance or exit. As we both stared at the dusty, rocky scene below, our eyes met in silent understanding. We both now realized how we could capture the illusive white stallion.

CHAPTER 24

HE NOW WAS MINE

We now felt as if we were on a mission. For the next couple of hours, we were relentless in our search for the horse. We rode until we found the other side of the gorge or what we thought was the other side. We checked up and down the hillside looking for tracks or any sign that the horse had passed this way. Even though the soil was very hard and rocky, and we found no trail, we felt he must still be in the ravine.

As we moved into the narrow valley, we sensed an excitement. He must be in here, we thought to ourselves. It wasn't long before we were proven right. The tight passageway opened into a wide space - and there he was. If this was the same gorge as on the other side of the mountain, then he was trapped. I got off Darlin' and handed the reins to Okomi to hold the horses. The entrance was now blocked tightly with the three horses standing side-by-side. I took the rope I had intended to use on him before and began to swing it over my head. The stallion began to pace back and forth, standing tall on his hind legs, and throwing his front legs high into the air. Just as I began to move closer, he turned and headed for the passage on the other side of the opening. I raced behind him. I couldn't see him anymore as he disappeared among the twists and turns of the gorge. I could still hear his hooves echoing through the ravine - and then - silence.

I stopped and listened. Did he escape again? Had he found another way out? Where did he go? Then all of a sudden, I heard snorting and the pounding of hooves getting louder. I quickly climbed a small ledge a few feet off the ground and I saw him coming - full throttle. Hooves flailing the ground into huge clouds of dust, his mane whipping in the wind, his nostrils wide and snorting with sounds like thunder. He was almost to me, and I instinctively jumped to grab him. I did it! I was on his back, and he picked up speed as he tried to run me off his back. My hands were full of his flowing mane, my heels were pressed, gripping tightly to his flank. We approached the open area again, and he tried to race to escape, but Okomi was there, blocking any attempt by him to get away. As he saw the exit blocked, he slowed enough for me to lash the rope around his neck. I did it just in time, as he now was kicking his front legs high, trying to throw me to the ground. My hands were knotted tightly in the rope and in his mane and I told myself there was no way he was going to throw me off.

I was not sure how long the battle lasted. He continued to run around in circles and buck and toss his body from side to side. He tried to scrape me off by running close to the sides of the canyon. He reared high into the air and then he would kick his hind legs, trying to shake me from his back. I knew that once I had him in my grip, there would be no way I would lose him now. He continued to fight, but I could tell the fight was wearing him down. Then as quickly as the battle started, it ended. He stopped resisting and stood calmly and quietly in the center of that canyon floor. He slowly pawed the ground in long strokes, and he began to fling his powerful neck up and down as if it was a sign of surrendering. I had won! He was mine! I leaned my head over to place my ear against his strong neck. On the side of my face, I could feel the sweat that had foamed on his white coat. I placed my arms around him and stroked him. As I paused there to soak up the thrill of success, I heard Okomi clapping his hands as it echoed through the mountain pass. I felt this was the greatest day of my life.

CHAPTER 25

TRIUMPHANT RIDE HOME

I did not need a saddle for my horse. I had learned to ride bareback from Okomi. I really wanted to ride him into town so everyone could see what I had done: I had captured the "wild one", the one everyone said could never be caught, never be tamed, and never be ridden - the one Thomas said did not even exist!

I still did not have a name for him. I wanted something that had meaning and would be important to me. Many names crossed my mind - Blaze, Lightning, Thunder, Sky, Beauty, Whitey and many more, but they did not have meaning to me. I was in no hurry to name him. I knew a name would come to me in time. All I cared about now was getting home with my new horse and seeing my family.

In the distance, I could see an old stagecoach marker. I could barely read the faded words that said "Ringgold - 15 miles". As we approached it, I stopped to tell Okomi that this was my town. It seemed he knew already. As I turned around to tell him, he was not riding next to me. He had stopped several yards back. He raised his hand to me as to say, "goodbye". Immediately, I got a sinking feeling in my stomach and a lump in my throat. I realized that Okomi would not come into town with me. I felt like I owed him so much. As I thought about him riding back to Oklahoma by himself, I decided to give him the rest of the rations we had from the Crossing. I pulled Princess up close to him and said, "Yours", and I handed him the reins.

He hesitated, with a puzzled look on his face and then he smiled and took the reins from me. At that moment, he reached into a little pouch he had tied around his waist. I had noticed it before, but I never asked what it was, and he never opened it the whole trip. Out of it he pulled a feather and a lace of leather with an eagle's claw tied in the middle. He handed me the claw and motioned me to put it around my neck. As I did it, he took the feather and looked at it intently. I saw a small smile come across his mouth. He did not put it in his headband. He slowly placed it back in his pouch. I figured he would save that moment when he got back to his village. It would probably be a special ceremony when the Chief would do the honor of putting it in his hair.

When he looked up, he raised his hand to me, and I offered mine to shake. We shook hands for what seemed a long time. It was as if we did not want our time together to end. Without one word spoken, he turned and headed east, back home, with Princess in tow. He would return to his village after a long journey, his quest completed; a hero to his people.

As I watched him trot off into the distance, I noticed he never looked back. I reached up to my neck and rubbed the claw between my finger and thumb.

"Thank you," I whispered to myself, "Thank you, my friend and brother."

I realized he had been on a mission - a mission to see me safely home. With his mission completed, he had earned his feather. "God's speed," I added, "I hope to see you again," and he was soon over the horizon.

Now, I turned my attention to getting home as quickly as I could. I had so much to tell my family and friends. As I relived all the adventures in my head, I wondered if anyone would believe me. They did not believe the stories I told them about my dad. Why would they believe anything about me? Maybe I wouldn't tell anyone any of my stories after all. All they needed to know was about the horse.

I crossed the rise and there it was, my home. Three months since I left. I could see Daniel out in the yard. He was chasing the chickens that had escaped the coop once again. Then I saw my mom, and she was chasing Daniel. They didn't see me yet. Even if they did, they would probably not have recognized the horse. As I got closer, I saw they had stopped running. They noticed a rider heading for their front gate. I saw mom shade her eyes, and then I saw her raise her arms over her head and she started to wave them frantically. Daniel ran toward me. At least I thought it was Daniel.

No, wait. It was Carrie all along, and she had been wearing pants! She had grown so much, she looked as big as Daniel! Now, I saw Daniel come out of the house and he took off running straight for me, full speed. He, too, had grown so much! Both were much bigger than I remembered. I could hear them calling my name, and I climbed off the horse. Carrie leaped into my arms as Daniel threw his arms around my waist and hugged me tightly. Mom was now in front of me. Her whole countenance was beaming. She reached for me and placed her hands on either side of my face and gave me a big kiss on my forehead.

"Billy," she said, with tears in her eyes, giving me a great big hug, "we have been waiting for you, and we are so glad you are home!"

At the same time, Carrie and Daniel were talking to me, too, and I couldn't hear what one was saying while the other was jabbering away. I heard words like, "outlaws," "Indians", "horse", "reward". I was having a hard time making out what anyone was saying as they all were trying to tell me something at the same time.

I looked in all their faces, and I was so proud to be home and to be with my family. I only wished dad was here, too. I never realized how much I missed them while I was gone. Mom took one arm; Carrie was squeezing my other hand tightly and Daniel had his arm around my waist as we walked toward the house. As Daniel and Carrie continued to chatter incessantly, Mom told them,

"Sh-h-h! He can't hear all of you at the same time! You will each have a chance to talk with him soon, but first Mother has to talk to him."

As I looked at my mom walking beside me, I thought maybe I have grown, too. I felt taller. I was taller! I could now look her straight in the eye. I tried to focus on what she had to tell me.

"Billy, we have heard so many stories about you."

About me? *How,* I thought. *Who would tell? What did they tell?* I thought about the stories concerning my dad. I thought how very few people around here believed them. I thought about how people would lie and make the stories into some tall tale, so unbelievable, people would laugh at my dad. I dreaded to hear what stories were being told about *me.* Whatever stories my mom had heard did not seem to bother her. Her face was still glowing and radiant.

"We heard about the outlaws at the Crossing . . . "

"Yeah," Daniel interrupted, "and how you got'm and tied'm up and saved'm for the Marshal, and the reward, and . . ."

"Daniel, you will have your turn," she admonished. "We heard about the Indian village and . . ."

"Yeah," he interrupted again, "and about the Indian chief and..."

"Daniel!" she scolded, and continued. "And we heard about Captain Watson . . ."

"You saved his life, didn't you, Billy, didn't you?" Daniel could not contain himself and interrupted for the third time. "You saved his life and the longhorns and all the men, didn't you, Billy?" I didn't think I had ever heard Daniel talk so much. I was not only surprised at how talkative he was, but how excited he was to see me and to hear my stories. This time, Mom did not fuss at him, and just let him talk.

"Well, it's a long story," I replied, almost feeling a little embarrassed to be the center of all this attention.

Daniel continued his deluge of words, "Everybody is talking about you, Billy. Everybody in town knows what you did. Everybody thinks you are the biggest hero they know."

I was now at a loss for words.

We were finally at the house, and we all sat on the front steps, huddled close together; mom on my right, Daniel on my left and Carrie, listening very quietly, at my feet.

"Tell us all about it, Billy. Tell us everything you did! Please, Billy, please!" begged Daniel.

I looked at all their faces as they eagerly anticipated my stories. For once I felt like I could tell them and someone would listen and believe.

For the rest of the afternoon and until late in the evening, I told the story about my adventure. They were captivated, hanging on every word I said. I told them about Clark and how he ran away from home to ride with me, and how he saved my life in the flood. I told them about the outlaws at the Crossing and the Red River and Mr. Chisholm. I told them about Marshal Bass Reeves and how he helped us. I told them about Chief Little Raven and his village. I told them about Captain John J. Watson and his cattle drive, and how Clark left with him, and I told them about Jake. I told the story about Okomi and the friendship we made and how we captured the white horse. By the time we finished, the sun was setting low in the west, and it was time to start supper. Daniel still had many questions. I had asked how they knew about many of my stories, and they said that Marshal Reeves had passed through town to pick up the two criminals Clark and I captured at the bank, and he told the Sheriff and the Sheriff told *everybody*.

Mom said, "If a Marshal told those stories then they must be true, so everybody believed him."

I told them I was feeling tired, and they all said they understood. As they went into the house, I took the horses to the barn and gave them feed and water. The beautiful white horse was not as restless as I expected him to be. He seemed content in the stable and was glad to eat and drink. I looked him in the eye and said, "Tomorrow we will ride again."

As I entered the house, I stretched and placed my hands in my back pockets. I felt something and I pulled out the envelope from the Marshall that Mr. Chisholm had given me back at the Crossing. I walked into the house with the rest of my family and sat at the table while Mom was finishing supper. I opened the letter, and out fell a bank note for $200.00 payable to "Master William Pecos, Esq." , and it said "FOR CAPTURE OF WANTED OUTLAWS." As I sat fixated on the money, Mom gave me another letter and said, "This is from the Sheriff for you. I was saving it."

Another one? I opened it, and it, too, had a bank note for the same amount - $200.00! And it *too* said, "FOR CAPTURE OF WANTED OUTLAWS".

"And, Billy," Mom continued, as she had been looking over my shoulder, "that's not all. The bank gave you a reward of $100.00, too." She laid the money in front of me.

I did not know what to say. Daniel had brought in my saddlebags, and I remembered the money I got for the cattle. I reached in and took out the envelope for the cattle I sold to Captain Watson. My mom watched as I counted out $1,300 for the longhorns.

"Billy!" she exclaimed. "I can't believe all of this fortune! Your father would be so proud of you!"

I thought to myself, *I believe he would be proud of me, too.*

CHAPTER 26

THE HOMECOMING

The next morning was Sunday, and my mom roused me out of bed. I had lost track of what day of the week it was. I really wanted to sleep in, but my mom insisted I go to church with the family. She made a big fuss over me about my clothes, and how I looked and how my hair was combed. She was usually making a fuss over the little ones, not me. She had made me a new shirt, and she had bought me a new pair of breeches with nice suspenders. She said she was glad she made the shirt a little larger, or it would not have fit me, in view of the fact that I had grown so much. And she said I would soon outgrow the pants she bought since they were now a perfect fit, and I would probably be growing a lot more. I don't know what the commotion was all about, but my family seemed to be so excited to be going to church this morning.

I was glad to see ol' Whiskers as I hitched him up to the wagon. I checked on Darlin' and the stallion, and they seemed fine. I was startled for a moment not seeing Princess, but then I remembered I gave her to Okomi.

I called the family, loaded them in the wagon, and we were soon off the church. I had a strange feeling as we rode into town. Folks I had never seen in church before were passing us. As everyone rode by, they were all smiling and waving and watching us as they drove their wagons around us. It seemed like everyone was in hurry to get to church today. The closer we got to it, the more people we saw flooding past us. Once we came into sight of the church, I was shocked to see so many buggies and wagons and horses and people standing everywhere and children running here and there.

"Are we having dinner-on-the-grounds today or something?" I asked my mom, "I haven't seen this many people since the last picnic at church and there weren't this many then. This crowd is huge."

"As a matter of fact," she answered, "we are."

"But we did not bring any food!" I screeched.

"This is a little different today, Billy," she said. I glanced at her, hoping she would explain what she meant, but she started looking around at all the people and began waving at them all. I felt like I was in a parade, as all eyes seemed to be on us. As we pulled up to park the wagon, everyone started to gather around us. Suddenly I got the feeling we were not here just for church.

As I pulled the wagon to a stop, I looked up to see a mass of people and then, in the midst of them, a banner was raised that said, "WELCOME HOME BILLY OUR HERO!" As the banner was lifted, it was as if it was a signal for everyone to let out a cheer. I had never heard that much noise at church before. Everyone was cheering and clapping and waving, and I couldn't believe what I was seeing and hearing. A couple of men helped my mom down off the wagon, and they helped Daniel and Carrie, too. I started to get down, but four men reached for me. Two took my legs the other two reached for my arms and they placed me on the shoulders of the first two. Now I was riding high above the crowd. I was overwhelmed. I couldn't believe what was happening. They took me into the church, and, as we went through the entrance, I had to duck to avoid hitting my head on the door frame. They took me to the front and lowered me near the pulpit. There was a single chair in the middle. As I stood and turned around, several men motioned to me to sit in the chair, which I did. The clapping and cheering and waving and noise continued as I sat and looked at the crowd that was now gathering in the pews. Everyone was standing, and, as soon as the last ones were entering the building, I saw the Sheriff and Mr. Turnipseed standing before the crowd and motioning for them to sit and to quiet down.

Mr. Turnipseed moved to my right and the Sheriff was on my left. The Sheriff began to speak.

"Ladies and gentlemen, we welcome home a true hero today - Young William Pecos."

The people in the pews again erupted in applause and cheers, but the Sheriff raised his hand to quite them so he could continue.

He now turned to me and said, "Billy, the town never got a chance to thank you for what you did before you left on your cattle drive: the night you saved Clark Turnipseed's life and saved this town's money." Again, the crowd cheered.

"And," the Sheriff said as he raised his hand again for silence, "the Mayor, the town council and the business leaders of this town want to give you this token of our appreciation." He handed me a small envelope. "Open it," he insisted.

As I opened it, I heard him tell me so all the audience could hear, "We all wanted you to have this."

When I opened it, it was just a simple note that said Thank you.

I looked up a little puzzled, but everyone before me had big grins on their faces. Then I saw the crowd step aside and part. There in front of me, draped over the pew, was the Mr. Ledbetter's beautiful black leather saddle that sat in Mr. Jacob's General Store.

"This is for you, Billy," the Sheriff said. I was still overwhelmed.

Then I heard someone yell from the back, "Speech!" Then I heard another and then a chorus of voices yelling, "Speech! Speech!"

I rose to my feet, and the noise immediately ceased. I could have heard a pin drop in that church. I cleared my throat, and I wondered where to begin.

"Thank you," was all I could collect to say at first, and, again, there was applause and cheering. The Sheriff, who had now been seated, stood to quiet the crowd again. "Let the boy speak!" he chided the people.

I looked at my mom, and she was crying. She was using her same hanky to wipe away tears from her cheeks. I knew they were tears of joy for me. All the faces of everyone were glued on me as I looked around the congregation. Just as I was about to start, I saw one of the church doors open. I saw Mrs. Turnipseed enter, as Charles held open the other of the great double doors. I then saw Samantha enter, sitting in her wheelchair, being pushed down the aisle by Britt.

She came right up to the front and stopped next to her dad, Mr. Turnipseed. She was looking at me, smiling ear to ear. She was wearing a beautiful white dress that seemed to flow around her, and again I thought I was seeing an angel. I was so glad to see her. I was looking at her and thinking of a thousand things to say to her. I then heard her father clear his throat and I quickly looked back at all the people. They were still waiting for me to speak.

"First," I started, "I want to tell the Turnipseeds that Clark is fine." I saw the whole family breathe a sigh of relief. "He has turned into quite a cowboy. You should see him in his denims and wide-brimmed hat rounding up those longhorns." I heard a light chuckle from the crowd. In a more serious tone, I added, "He is a real hero, Mr. Turnipseed. You should be very proud of him. Had it not been for Clark, I would have been close to dying out there on the trail."

Mr. Turnipseed smiled and I watched as tears welled up in his eyes.

"Second, I want to thank my mom and my siblings for loving me and waiting for me and believing in me." I looked down at them sitting on the front pew, "I knew your thoughts and prayers were with me, and that remembrance kept me going."

"Third, I want to thank my dad. I never saw him on this trip, but his spirit and his good will was all around me every day. I love him, and I am so proud of him, and I can't wait until he comes home."

"And, fourth, I want to thank you, the people of Ringgold, for this wonderful gift, and I have just the horse for it." There was a loud and quick cheer.

"And most of all I want to thank God for watching over me and protecting me the whole time."

Then someone from the crowd hollered to me, "Whatcha' gonna do with all that reward money you got, Billy?" The crowd buzzed for a moment.

"That's a good question." I paused as everyone chuckled, and then said, "I will take care of my family first; and then," I looked directly at my mom, "if it's alright with you, Mom, I want to go to college, maybe back East, like Clark and study like he did."

Someone in the back yelled, "The banker became the cowboy, and you'll become the banker!" And with that, the whole congregation burst out in laughter. Then as I sat down, the crowd stood and applauded.

The rest of the morning was full of good cheer from everyone, and they all wanted to greet me and repeat the stories to me that they had heard about my adventures. And many who had heard the stories, wanted to hear it from me firsthand. A plate of food had been shoved into my hands, but I had no time to eat.

I could not remember the number of times I told each story. I did not mind telling them over and over. Everyone was so excited to hear me talk. Older people would tell me how I was like my dad. Younger people offered to travel with me whenever I wanted to strike out again. Children quizzed me again and again about every intricate detail of what had happened. Amid all the hullabaloo, two figures walked up to me and I was surprised to see them. It was Thomas and Silas.

"I knew he was out there all along, but I never thought anyone would catch him, especially you," Thomas said as he glared at me.

"Yeah, and I was the one who wanted that saddle," added Silas, stone-faced.

As my eyes darted back and forth between the two – not sure what would happen next - I watched as grins creeped across their faces.

"You're a good cowboy, Billy. Come by and show me that horse one day," Thomas said as he reached out to shake my hand.

"I want to sit on that saddle one day. Will you let me, Billy?" added Silas as he patted me on the shoulder.

I smiled back. "Sure. Sounds fine to me."

Before they could get out of the way, Elizabeth Todd had pushed past Thomas and Silas to the front of the church. She appeared as bossy as ever. "I knew that you could do it. I told everyone, 'If someone was going to get that horse, Billy Pecos could,' and I was right – as always." With that, she pranced off with her long curls flying.

At that moment, I saw the crowd around me part as Britt pushed Samantha up to me. I knelt in front of her and she spoke first.

"I'm glad you're home. Will you come and see me soon?"

"Yes," I quickly replied, "Yes, I will, very soon!"

"And show me your new horse?"

"Yes, I will."

"Do you have a name for him yet?" she asked.

As I looked at Samantha, I suddenly thought of the name I would give my great, white stallion.

"His name is Sam!"

www.ingramcontent.com/pod-product-compliance
Lightning Source LLC
Chambersburg PA
CBHW051137020726
47501CB00005B/1554